# When Skies are Gray

For Kylee & Elisa
Enjoy! Blessings
on both of you —
Leanne Lucas

2022

# Endorsements

Leanne Lucas's *When Skies Are Gray* is a blast of pure sunshine. Lucas grapples with big issues, including impending war, a Depression, and family struggles. But rays of light always manage to slip through the clouds, thanks to her delightful protagonist, a young girl named Lizzy. With glimmers of *Little Women*, Lizzy, her siblings, and her cousins confront their trials with courage and hope—but not in a saccharine way. Amid the mounting troubles, Lucas shows a deep understanding of the power of family and faith. I highly recommend *When Skies Are Gray*. It will light up your day.
—**Doug Peterson**, historical novelist and former *VeggieTales* writer

In her latest novel, *When Skies Are Gray*, Leanne Lucas has penned a story full of mystery, childhood secrets, and Christian values, all within the warm and engaging Richter family. A wonderful book for middle-grade readers.
—**Kay DiBianca**, award-winning author of *The Watch* mystery series

*When Skies are Gray* is a story about trust, forgiveness, and hope. Lucas sets the story in small-town Illinois with the Richter family. It is the end of the Great Depression, and the Richters find themselves in the middle of a family conflict. Lucas's rich development of characters and plot twists keep the reader wondering the fate of the family as well as the bonds that will keep them connected. An excellent historical fiction that connects the themes of love and loyalty.

—**Andrea Bear**, author of *Grieving Daughters' Club*

*When Skies Are Gray* is a heartwarming novel you won't want to put down until you've reached the end. The story reminds us of what is good, true, and worthy of sacrifice.

—**Carol Schlorff**, author of the upcoming middle-grade novel *How to Kill a Giant*

I love how historically accurate the story is, and the relationships between the cousins make them lovable and beautiful characters. *When Skies Are Gray* is an engaging and fun read, displaying redemption and Christ's love.

—**Mary U.**, age 12

# When Skies Are Gray

## Leanne Lucas

A Christian Company
ElkLakePublishingInc.com

# Copyright Notice

Cover: Lana Ziegler, Derinda Babcock
Interior Design: Deb Haggerty
Editor(s): Mel Hughes, Deb Haggerty

PUBLISHED BY: Elk Lake Publishing, Inc., 35 Dogwood Drive, Plymouth, MA 02360, 2022

---

**Library Cataloging Data**

Names: Lucas, Leanne (Leanne Lucas)
*When Skies are Gray* / Leanne Lucas

202 p. 23cm × 15cm (9in × 6 in.)

ISBN-13: 978-1-64949-772-7 (paperback) | 978-1-64949-773-4 (trade hardcover) | 978-1-64949-774-1 (trade paperback) | 978-1-64949-775-8 (e-book)

Key Words: Christian children's fiction, historical fiction, Great Depression, German families, shell shock, PTSD; family relationships; faith

# Dedication

For my husband, David

Your steadfast commitment and your constant encouragement keep me focused on the work God has set before me. Your wacky sense of humor makes it all more fun than I could ever have imagined.

# Acknowledgments

Many thanks to my beta readers, Terri Elder and Mary Underhill. Your comments and suggestions gave me fresh insight and much-needed encouragement.

My deepest thanks to my editor, Mel Hughes. Your expertise and your thoughtful suggestions made this a much better book.

My sincere appreciation to Deb Haggerty, Cristel Phelps, Derinda Babcock, and everyone at Elk Lake Publishing, Inc. Your patience and guidance have made this publishing experience entirely enjoyable.

Finally, my love and gratitude to the family members who lived through this time period and shared their memories with me. My late parents, Wayne and Betty Hilst, my stepmother, Norma Jean Bilyeu Hilst, and my aunts, Pat Wilson and Betty Joy Christians, are exemplary members of the "greatest generation."

# Chapter One

Lizzy was the only one who heard the voice—far away, a familiar shout, nothing more. She splashed to the bank of the Dinky Ditch. The November sun teased the back of her neck with its faint warmth, but it had no effect on the chilly water that rippled and swirled down the creek bed. She shivered when she stepped onto the large, cold rock the girls used as a stepping stone into the stream.

Lizzy glanced at her sister Ginny and her cousin Marianne to see if they had heard the voice. She put a finger to her lips. "Shhh." Neither paid attention to her.

The two girls stood in the middle of the stream. Their blond heads touched as they hunched over to look for guppies. Both of them had their skirts pulled up and tucked between their legs to keep their hems out of the water. Marianne gave the goosebumps that dotted her legs a vigorous rub.

Ginny reached out and grasped Marianne's arm. "Hold real still."

Marianne froze.

"The secret to catching guppies," Ginny continued, "is don't *try* to catch them. Cup your hands and wait for them to swim to you."

She pushed Marianne's hands underwater. They both leaned forward and almost tipped over. A school of guppies streamed past.

Marianne gave up and splashed over to join Lizzy on the bank. "What's the matter? You look funny."

"I thought I heard a voice. Listen."

Marianne cocked her head and concentrated. "I don't hear anything. Can you catch a guppy?"

"What would I do with a guppy?"

Marianne grinned. "Give him to me."

"What would *you* do with him?"

"Nothing. Throw him back. I just want to see what one feels like."

"They're wiggly and slimy." Lizzy wiped her feet on the dry, brown grass. "Let's get our shoes and socks on. We have to get Opa's stuff and get home before dark."

She took her cousin by the hand and pulled her up the steep bank. A tumble of book bags, shoes, and socks were dumped near the road. Lizzy pulled Marianne's socks out of the pile. She glanced down the bank. Ginny stood knee-deep in the water.

Lizzy cupped her hands around her mouth. "Come on, Ginny. Get out and get your shoes and socks on." She nudged the jumble with her toe to find her own socks. "Where's Elinor?"

"Right here." Elinor, so close her breath tickled Lizzy's ear, laughed when Lizzy jumped. She had her hands cupped together, and she held them out to Lizzy. "Look at this."

Lizzy took a step back. "Don't tell me you caught a guppy."

"No, I didn't get in the creek. I wanted to catch butterflies."

Elinor opened her hands. A plain yellow butterfly trembled briefly in her palm before flying a confused path to the water's edge.

"They're so graceful." Elinor waved her arms in a gentle imitation of the butterfly. "I wish I was that graceful."

Lizzy tugged Elinor's arms back to her side. Only Elinor understood Elinor's fascination for butterflies, and the dance would go on forever if Lizzy didn't stop her. "Did you hear that voice?"

Elinor shook her head. "What voice?"

"Never mind." Lizzy turned back to the ditch. "Ginny!"

Ginny waded through the water to the bank. "It won't get dark for another hour. Why do we have to leave now?"

"Because we have to get Opa's stuff. Then we have to get home and get our homework done. Mama won't let you listen to *Fibber McGee and Molly* tonight if you don't have your homework done."

Ginny scrambled up the incline on all fours and grabbed her shoes and socks. "I forgot. Why didn't you remind me?"

"I just did."

Ginny took two steps down the gravel road before Lizzy's sharp voice stopped her. "Put on your shoes and socks."

Ginny made a face but she plopped down on the dirt road next to Marianne. She pulled on the once-white socks and her hand-me-down saddle shoes. She didn't tie the shoes, and Lizzy didn't fight her.

The four cousins trooped down the dirt road to Hobbs Hill, the inflated name for a mild rise in the flat farm country of east-central Illinois. They crested the hill, and there was Opa's house, the only one on the lonesome stretch of road. Cornfields, harvested and tilled, surrounded the home, waiting for the first snow.

They were almost to Opa's lane when a black streak raced around the far corner of the house. A large dog barreled towards them. Lizzy reached out to pull the two younger girls behind her.

But Marianne loved dogs as much as her sister loved butterflies, and she ducked away from Lizzy's protective reach as the dog approached.

"It's okay." Marianne pointed. "Look at his tail."

The tail, black with a white tip, beat side-to-side in a blur.

Marianne waited until the dog was close. Then she held out her hand and pointed at the ground. "Sit."

The dog skidded to a stop. Then he sat. His tail still beat back and forth.

Marianne clapped. "Good dog!" The mutt jumped up and ran in circles around her. She pulled him to a stop and scratched his head and rubbed his ears. "Where did you come from?"

Lizzy was wondering the same thing. She looked down the lane, searching for someone who might belong to the dog. Someone she might have heard earlier. There was no one in sight. The dog was friendly enough, but he didn't look well cared for or well fed. "He's probably a stray."

Elinor wrinkled her nose. "That is one smelly dog. Don't encourage him. You know Ma won't let you have a dog in the house."

Marianne wasn't listening. She whispered in the dog's ear. He licked her face with a long, rough tongue, and she giggled.

Elinor shook her head and started up the lane. The others followed. The black dog stayed with them, pressed to Marianne's side. He knew a kindred spirit when he met one.

Everyone grew quiet as they approached the house. Weeds filled the flowerbeds bordering the front porch. There was one red rose left on a scraggly bush, protected by vicious-looking thorns. A curtain hung crooked in the front window, and dry leaves skittered across the porch floor.

Ginny voiced what they were all thinking. "I wish Opa still lived here."

Lizzy found the key to the house in a notch in one of the porch beams. "Well, he doesn't. He can't." She jiggled the doorknob and realized the door was unlocked. The ugly dog was at her side, and the hinges squeaked as he pushed past her and into the house.

Lizzy grabbed at his matted fur, but the dog was strong, and he sped through the house to the kitchen before she could stop him. Marianne chased after him, with Lizzy close behind.

The dog was sniffing his way around the baseboards of the kitchen cabinets. When he came to the door to the cellar, he sat down and looked at Lizzy with hopeful eyes.

Lizzy shook her head. "No way. There's nothing down there but last year's potatoes." She turned to Marianne. "Take him out the back door, would you? I don't think Opa would want him in the house."

Marianne gave a sharp clap. "Come on, Brutus. Let's go play fetch."

"Brutus?"

"I'm going to call him Brutus."

"Fine. Please take Brutus outside."

Brutus was reluctant to cooperate, but Marianne coaxed and whistled and finally pulled the dog out the back door and down the steps.

Lizzy glanced around the kitchen. There were two plates, a glass, a cup and saucer, and several forks and spoons laid out on the sideboard.

Elinor leaned against the kitchen door. "At least Opa did his dishes before he left."

Lizzy shook her head. "I don't think so. Those dishes weren't there when Gene and I came out a couple weeks ago."

A loud clatter from the living room startled both girls. Ginny's muffled voice floated down the hall. "It's okay. I just dropped the *Scrabble* board. Somebody's playing— well, somebody was playing *Scrabble*."

Elinor shrugged. "Maybe it was the same person who did the dishes. Weren't the twins out here last week?"

Lizzy laughed. "The twins? Playing *Scrabble* and doing dishes? I don't think so."

More clattering from the living room, then a loud, frustrated sigh. "Lizard! Should I pick up the *Scrabble* tiles?"

Lizzy closed her eyes and counted to three before she spoke. "Yes, Ginny, since you dropped the *Scrabble* tiles, you should pick up the *Scrabble* tiles. Pack everything in the box, and find the *Monopoly* game as well. Opa wants us to bring them both home."

A long silence from the living room. Then, "All right."

Elinor, queen of the eye roll, listened to the exchange. "Were we ever that annoying?" She didn't wait for an answer. "What else does Opa need?"

"A flannel shirt, his almanac, and his good pipe. I think that's it. He said those things are in his bedroom."

Lizzy walked down the hall to the bedroom and opened the door. She stopped short.

Opa's bed was made but the covers were rumpled, as if someone had been taking a nap. There was a cup half-full of coffee next to an open Bible face-down on the night stand.

Elinor walked into the room. "One of the twins made themselves at home."

Lizzy shook her head. *I don't think so. Both twins gripe when they have to read the Bible for Sunday school. Neither one of them would ever read it on their own.*

Lizzy heard the unkind words in her head and took a breath. *Sorry, Lord. That wasn't nice. But—well, you know I'm right.*

Lizzy picked up the Bible and glanced at the open page. Psalm 119. Someone had underlined verse 97. "O, how I love thy law! It is my meditation all the day."

*Nope. Definitely not one of the twins.* She snapped the Bible shut and set it on the nightstand. "Let's just get Opa's stuff and get out."

The top drawer stuck when she pulled on the knob. She pulled again and almost dumped the drawer's contents on the floor. An intricate carved pipe rested next to a full bag of pipe tobacco. Opa's almanac and a Zane Grey novel, *Riders of the Purple Sage*, were shoved in the back. Both books were dog-eared from use. Lizzy pulled out the novel and thumbed it open.

"Zane Grey is one of Gene's favorites. Opa won't mind if he reads this." She stuffed the book, the almanac, and the pipe in the bag that hung from her shoulder.

"What else?" Elinor asked.

Lizzy pointed to the hall tree in the corner. Elinor pulled a blue flannel shirt off one of the hooks.

Lizzy gave a troubled glance around the room before she pulled the door shut behind her. "Come on. You go out the back door and get Marianne. I'll lock up and meet you out front."

Lizzy found Ginny in the living room reading the *Monopoly* box. "Let's go." She led the way out the front door. She turned the knob to make sure the door was locked and put the key back in the porch post.

Marianne and Brutus ran around the corner of the house with Elinor close behind. Marianne saw the games. "We have *Monopoly,* but I've never played *Scrabble.* Can I carry the box? Please, Ginny?"

"Okay." Ginny handed the game to her cousin. "Be careful."

Marianne stuck the box out for Brutus to sniff, and he obliged. "Maybe I'll teach Brutus how to play."

"You can't keep the dog." Elinor's voice was sharp. "You know Ma won't let you."

Marianne's bottom lip trembled. "I'm still going to ask." She stomped ahead of them with Brutus by her side. Ginny caught up with her, and they walked up the lane with the dog between them, each with a free hand on his back.

Brutus, unaccustomed to such devoted attention, darted to the side of the road to sniff through a clump of weeds. He ran back just as quickly and nudged his way to his place between the girls, causing them both to giggle and stumble.

"Ginny, you're going to drop the *Monopoly* box in the dirt if you're not careful." Lizzy called out to her sister when Ginny came to an abrupt halt.

Herta Mueller sat on her bike at the top of Hobbs Hill, blocking their path. She was a hefty girl with a single dirty blonde braid, squinty eyes, and a pinched face. She tipped the bike to one side and reached down to the road. She straightened up and began pitching rocks at Ginny.

"Take this." Lizzy shoved her bag at Elinor. She ran up the hill and straight for Herta.

Herta tried to back up but Lizzy was too fast for her. Lizzy grabbed the handlebars and shook them. "Stop throwing rocks at my sister. What are you doing here?"

"What's wrong with you?" Herta dropped the rocks. "I didn't hit 'em. Let go of my bike!" She jerked the handlebars out of Lizzy's grasp. "What are *you* doing here?"

"We came to get a few things for my grandfather."

"I don't believe you. How do I know you're not stealing stuff? My dad's been watching this place, and I bet you're the ones he's been watching!"

Lizzy and Elinor exchanged a glance. Why was the town policeman watching Opa's house?

"We come out here all the time." Lizzy didn't think Opa's problems were Herta's business, so her explanation was brief. "Opa lives in town with us now, and he needs stuff."

Herta's frown deepened. "I still don't believe you. I think you're stealing. I'm gonna tell my dad."

Lizzy shrugged. "Go ahead."

Herta had one rock hidden in her hand. She pitched it at the younger girls and almost hit Brutus.

The dog growled low in his throat. Marianne patted Brutus on the head. "I'll sic my dog on you."

"He's not your dog." Herta's voice trembled.

Brutus barked sharply and crouched—ready to lunge.

Herta flipped her bike around and flew down the hill. Seconds later, she disappeared around the curve to Black Hawk Grove.

Brutus relaxed, and Marianne wrapped her arms around his neck. "Thanks, boy."

The girls followed Herta's dust trail down the road. They walked side by side, a picture of the nickname everyone used for them—the Stair Steps. Eleven years old, Lizzy was the oldest and the tallest. Elinor was a year younger and two inches shorter. Ginny, the third step down, came a year after Elinor, and Marianne was the youngest and the smallest. They all had different shades of blond hair, and their cornflower blue eyes were a family trait.

Brutus walked by Marianne's side all the way into town. The cousins stopped when they reached Elinor and Marianne's house. Elinor handed Lizzy the flannel shirt, and Marianne reluctantly gave up the *Scrabble* box. "Ask Opa when we can borrow this."

Ginny took the box. "Maybe we can play a game when we have family supper."

The Richter family supper happened at least twice a week. The four girls were not only best friends, they were also double cousins. Their mothers were sisters, and their fathers were brothers. Elinor and Marianne had four older brothers. Lizzy and Ginny had five. Their mothers liked to share the work to feed the thirteen kids whenever they could. Since Daddy had left, Lizzy knew Mama counted on family supper.

Marianne was trying to coax Brutus to the house, and Elinor stopped her one last time.

"You can't keep him!"

Marianne ignored her.

"He'll eat Gracie."

"Oh." Marianne sighed. Aunt Meg kept chickens, and in typical Marianne fashion, they all had names. Gracie was her favorite. She gave Brutus a final hug. "I guess you better go home."

Brutus nuzzled her hand, then turned and trotted back the way they had come.

The two sisters waved goodbye from their porch steps. Lizzy and Ginny continued down John Q Street. They were three houses from home when their front door banged open and Joe, the oldest twin, stepped out on the porch.

"Hurry up, slowpokes!" His voice carried down the street, magnified by excitement. "We've got a letter from Frank, and Mama won't open it until you get here!"

All thoughts of an unknown voice, Opa's messy bedroom, and pesky Herta fled. Lizzy clutched Opa's shirt to her chest. Her book bag slid off her shoulder and dangled on her elbow, banging against her leg. She ran flat out, with Ginny on her heels.

# Chapter Two

Lizzy and Ginny kicked off their shoes inside the front door. No one wore shoes in the house. Mama's polished wooden floors were her pride and joy. Lizzy dropped her school bag and Opa's shirt on the table in the hallway. Ginny's bag hit the floor, and she tossed the games on the table. They followed Joe through the dining room door where the rest of the family was gathered around the table.

Gene sat reading while Hank showed Opa an article in the *Black Hawk Grove Review*. Joe snatched a ginger snap cookie from the plate in front of his twin, Jack. Jack grabbed Joe's wrist, gave it a twist, and snatched the cookie back.

Opa watched the tussle. He reached out and took the cookie from Jack, then smacked Joe on the back of the head. "If you two don't stop fighting, I will deal with the both of you."

Joe muttered something under his breath, and Jack sighed, but they stopped. Lizzie grabbed a cookie and sat down.

Everyone grew quiet when Mama tapped the letter on the table. She opened Frank's letter the way she always did, carefully, slowly, with her pearl-handled letter opener. She slipped the pages out of the envelope and laid them on the table, smoothing them open with both hands.

The letter was two and-a-half pages long, written on both sides in Frank's small, neat handwriting.

Mama read through the first page, front and back, with deliberate care. She handed it to Opa. They always did this, to make sure there was nothing the girls shouldn't hear. Everyone waited while Opa stirred his coffee and read through the last page Mama handed him. Joe tried to sneak the ginger snap Jack had in front of him, but Hank saw him and gave him another head smack.

Opa looked up and winked at Mama. She smiled. All the children started talking at once.

"Is he done with boot camp?"

"Is he still on KP duty?"

"Is he coming home?"

*Please, Lord, please, please ...* Lizzy closed her eyes and waited.

"He's coming home."

The room exploded with whoops and hollers, and even Opa smiled.

Mama waited for them to quiet down. "He doesn't know the date yet, but his commanding officer told everyone they would get a ten-day pass before they shipped out."

"Only ten days?" Lizzy couldn't keep the disappointment from her voice.

Mama nodded. "That's more than I expected. Sometimes they don't let them come home at all before their first tour of duty."

Ginny frowned. "What does shipped out mean? Is he going to be on a ship? I thought only the navy soldiers were on ships."

"Frank's part of the navy," Hank told her. "He's a Marine, and Marines guard navy ships."

"Wonder where he'll be when the war comes?" Joe's question hung in the air.

Mama pushed her chair back and stood. "We're not in the war."

"Not yet." Joe's words were barely audible, and all the jubilation oozed out of the room.

Jack was the first to break the silence. He reached for another cookie. "We heard on the radio the Germans torpedoed one of our tankers and one of our destroyers, so Congress authorized our merchant ships to carry arms. You know what that means, don't you?"

Opa's face darkened like a thundercloud. "It don't mean nothin'."

"It means we'll fight back if they try again, and if that happens, we'll be at war with Germany. It's going to happen, Opa. You know it is." Jack was the stubborn twin.

Opa didn't answer, and Joe jumped into the conversation. "Hitler's moving fast, and if we don't do something soon, we'll all be goose-stepping Nazi krauts."

Opa slammed his spoon down. "Why do you say that, Joseph? By definition, *you* are a 'kraut.' Every person at this table is a 'kraut.'"

Joe refused to back down. "No, Opa, we're Germans. We're not Nazi krauts."

"And somebody has to stop Hitler," Jack added. "I hope it's us."

Opa closed his eyes. "Never hope for war. You've seen firsthand what war does to a man."

"Frank Junior is not his father." The steel in Mama's voice quieted the room. She snatched the cookie plate off the table. "Adversity can bring out the best in a man. I believe it will bring out the best in Frank." She stared at Opa. "And you should pray for your son, not belittle him."

All the anger faded from Opa's face. "Of course, Annie. I'm sorry."

Mama handed the last cookie to Lizzy and left the room without answering. Opa picked up his coffee cup and followed Mama into the kitchen.

Hank grabbed the letter and began reading. "Want to hear what he has to say?"

Joe chucked his older brother on the shoulder. "Don't be smart, just read it."

Ginny nudged Lizzy. "Can I have half your cookie?"

Lizzy snapped the cookie in two and gave Ginny the bigger half. She sucked on her half so the crunching wouldn't drown out Hank's voice.

> Hello Mama, Opa, all you rowdies, Lizzy, and Ginny,
>
> Well, boot camp is over in two days, and I'll be coming home! I can't wait to see all of you, even the twins.

Both twins smiled. Frank always gave them a hard time.

> I'll get my duty notice before leave starts, so I'll let you know where I'll be headed when I come home. I know Mama will be happy if I'm stateside. Wherever I go, I'm eager to get going on my military career. It's hard to listen to the news from Europe and know America isn't involved. But I've got a feeling that will change soon enough.

Lizzy took a shaky breath, and Hank stopped reading. He skimmed the first page, and she knew he was looking for something cheerful. He skimmed the next page and laughed.

> My bunkmate kept short-sheeting my bed, but I finally wised up. Now I check every night. Me and Livewire got him back last week. He's a pretty heavy sleeper, so one night we waited until he was snoring real good, then we shaved off one of his eyebrows. The drill sergeant saw him the next morning and made him shave the other one so he'd look balanced.

Everyone shouted with laughter, and Joe reached over to cover both of Gene's eyebrows. Mama and Opa came back in the room. Mama pointed at Joe. "Don't even think about shaving anyone's eyebrows."

Hank read the rest of the letter, filled with comments about Frank's daily routine and the men who trained with him. Frank always complained about boot camp food, telling Mama how much he missed her cooking. He knew she would smile, and she always did.

> Mama, all my love to you. Opa, take care of yourself. Hank, since you're in charge now, smack the twins, help Gene with his history project, and give the girls a kiss and a hug for me. Keep me in your prayers,
> Frank

Ginny gave a sigh of happiness. "I can't wait to show Frank my new knuckleball pitch."

Joe laughed. "You don't have a knuckleball pitch. Your hand's barely big enough to hold the ball."

Ginny stuck her tongue out. "I'm practicing every night, and Frank will help me."

Hank smacked Joe on the head with the letter and gave him a stern look. "She's learning."

"Yeah, yeah."

Mama took the letter from Hank. She followed the same routine every time they got a letter from Frank. She opened the long drawer on the hutch and tucked his newest letter on top of the others. She straightened them into a neat pile. Next, she straightened the photo of Daddy and the only two letters he had written when he first left. Finally, she patted the news clippings she kept, which now included Lizzy's essay published in the *Black Hawk Grove Review*.

She stepped back and shut the drawer with a bang. "Time to do homework. Supper's in an hour and if you're not finished, you can't listen to *Fibber McGee and Molly*."

Lizzy gave Ginny an "I told you so" look.

Ginny groaned. "But I've got a whole new spelling list to write out."

"Then you better get busy."

Hank reached over to tweak Ginny's nose to make her smile. "Hey, Squeaker, get your words done, and we'll play a game of *Monopoly* while we listen to the radio. What do you say?"

"I get to be the shoe."

"Battleship," called Joe and Jack at the same time.

Lizzy dawdled at the table until everyone left the dining room. She opened the hutch drawer. There was the essay she had written, all about Frank's time in boot camp. Mama cried when the editor of the *Review* chose "My Brother the Marine" for publication.

Lizzy was only interested in the letters from Daddy. She had read them both so many times she had them memorized. On top of the letters was the photo of Daddy and his best friend, Myron, in their service uniforms.

The photo had been taken before the two men left to fight the Great War in Europe, before Daddy had been shot and almost died, before Myron carried him to safety. Daddy only spoke of that battle one time, but remembering the harsh catch in his voice and the tears he didn't cry still gave Lizzy goosebumps. Myron had eventually died in the Great War. His grin in the picture always made Lizzy wish she could have met him.

She moved the photo aside and pulled out the top envelope. She wanted to check the end of Daddy's first letter.

Annie, all my love to you. Frank, you're in charge now, so keep the older boys in line, help Gene with his homework, and give the girls a kiss and a hug for me. Keep me in your prayers.

Lizzy swallowed a lump in her throat. The dining room door squeaked, and Gene poked his head in the room. Lizzy tried to slip the letter and the envelope back in the drawer without Gene noticing, but it was too late. He came to her side.

"Frank always sounds like Pops, don't you think?" All the boys called their father Pops, although Gene was the only one who spoke of him anymore.

"I guess." Lizzy swallowed hard. "There are times I can't—remember him."

Gene nodded. "Me, either." He pulled the envelope out and straightened the letter inside so it lay flat. "I used to check the mailbox every day for another letter. Or I'd sit on the porch after school, imagining him walking up the street swinging his lunchbox." He shut the hutch drawer with a soft thud. "Not anymore."

"He's *coming home*." Lizzy bit her lip, surprised at the passion in her words.

Gene's eyes flickered briefly with a hope that faded before it could take hold. "How can you believe that?"

*I believe it because he loves us. Because I pray and pray that God will bring him back. Because I can't believe he would leave us—forever.* She couldn't get those words to come out of her mouth. She rubbed her eyes with one hand. "Mama believes it. So do I."

"All Mama said was when Pops left, he told her he'd be back. She hasn't spoken about it since. That was two years ago." Gene turned to leave the room, and Lizzy knew the conversation was over. He reached the door and spoke over his shoulder. "Opa said you brought the *Scrabble* game home."

Lizzy pushed past Gene through the door. She got the box from the hall table and shoved it at her brother.

"Here." She pulled the pipe and the almanac out of her book bag and set them on the table next to Opa's shirt.

When she pulled out the Zane Grey novel, Gene plucked the book from her hand. "I love this one!"

Lizzy frowned. "You've already read it?"

"Yeah, this is one of ..." Gene stopped himself, then shrugged. "It's one of Pops' favorites. Were you going to read it?"

She shook her head. "No. I thought you might want to. I guess not."

"Are you kidding? I always read books twice." He thumbed through the well-worn pages, then flipped to the first chapter. "I'll read this tonight—unless you need help with your homework."

Lizzy shook her head. "I don't have any, but don't tell Mama." Mama would make her help Ginny with her spelling, and the little twerp always got sloppy and whiny after the first few words.

She carried her book bag up the stairs to the room she and Ginny shared. She plopped down on the bed, lay back, and took a deep breath. Her insides were still quivery from her talk with Gene. Sometimes, she went days without thinking about Daddy. When she did think about him, her stomach always jellied up like it was doing now. She closed her eyes.

*Please, Lord, I hate feeling like this. I hate feeling like I should give up. I don't want to give up on Daddy, but even Gene is starting to doubt ...* A tear leaked out and rolled down her cheek. She brushed it away. *No. I'm not giving up. Please bring him home, Lord, please ...*

She pushed herself up and off the bed. *Okay, I've prayed, and I know God heard me. That's all I can do.* She grabbed her book bag off the floor. The only thing left inside was a Nancy Drew book. She pulled out the book, sat back on her bed, and willed herself to focus on Nancy, George, and Bess.

Ten minutes later, deep in *The Clue of the Tapping Heels*, she half-jumped out of her skin at a sharp knock on the door. No one ever knocked except Opa. What could he want?

"Come in."

Opa opened the door and peered inside. Several seconds of silence followed. Lizzy spoke first. "Hi, Opa."

Opa cleared his throat. "Hello, Elizabeth."

Uh-oh. Opa never called her Elizabeth unless something was wrong. Lizzy pulled herself to a sitting position and waited.

"Well." Opa cleared his throat again. "Well, let's see. I appreciate you girls going out to the house today to get my things." He looked at the floor. "But could you go back tomorrow?"

Lizzy relaxed. "Sure, Opa. What else do you need?"

Opa stepped back and looked up and down the hall before he answered. "I forgot to have you get my pipe tobacco. I'm running out."

Lizzy tried not to smile. Her mother had put Opa on a strict ration of "that evil weed." "Okay. What else?"

"Well, I got a bottle of tonic water in the bottom drawer of my dresser. Could you get that too?"

"Sure. What's tonic water?"

"Tonic keeps you from getting malaria."

"What's malaria?"

"A disease I don't wanna get."

Lizzy shrugged. "Okay." She'd look malaria up later. "Anything else?"

"Nope." Opa looked down the hall again. "Bring everything to my room when you get home."

"Okay."

"Straight to my room."

"Straight to your room."

Mama called from the bottom of the stairs. "Lizzy, come set the table."

Opa gave her a wink. "Thanks, Squirt."

\*\*\*

The next afternoon, Lizzy made the trip out to the farm alone. Ginny and Marianne had to stay after school to practice for the upcoming Armistice Day assembly. The third and fourth graders were singing "America the Beautiful," with Elinor accompanying them on piano.

Lizzy pulled her coat close around her. She left the road and walked through the corn stubble in the field above the Dinky Ditch. She searched the banks of the ditch, hoping to find something of interest. Once she had found a pair of shoes that fit Ginny. Another time she found a man's wallet, empty except for a worn photo of a woman and a small boy.

Today she saw a man's woolen cap floating in the water at the edge of the ditch, caught on a thistle bush. Lizzy slipped down the embankment and pulled the wet cap from the thorns.

She couldn't put the soggy hat in her pocket or her book bag, so she tucked it under the bush to pick up on her way home. The hat would fit Gene perfectly. He needed one for the coming winter. The hat he had now had holes and was beginning to unravel in the back.

She returned to the road and soon came to the fork in the road that turned into Opa's lane. Her step slowed as she approached the house. She'd never been to Opa's alone. *You probably didn't hear a voice. No one else heard a voice.*

Still, she couldn't seem to make her feet go any faster. *Grow up, scaredy-cat.* She picked up her pace and was halfway to the house when the front door opened. Brutus skidded across the porch and down the steps, barking a joyous greeting.

Lizzy barely saw the scrawny dog running toward her. *I locked the door yesterday. Who unlocked it?* A tall, lanky, familiar form filled the door. Frank! He was back! *Why is he at Opa's house?*

She didn't know, and she didn't care. She raced past the barking dog and ran the rest of the way to the house. She took the porch steps two at a time and was ready to throw herself into her brother's arms when she took a good look at his face. She stopped so quickly she almost fell backwards down the steps.

Strong arms reached out to catch her. "Hello, Lizzy," said her father.

# Chapter Three

Lizzy stared at Frank Richter, Sr. No. It couldn't be. Could it? Her thoughts were so jumbled, she squeezed her eyes shut to think. *Is this real, Lord? Are you really answering my prayers?*

She opened her eyes. Daddy was still there, his grip on her arm strong and familiar. Her legs felt like rubber. "What are you doing here?" Her voice cracked.

Daddy smiled. "Come inside, Squirt, and we'll talk."

For no reason she understood, Daddy's casual use of the familiar nickname made her furious and put strength back in her legs. She jerked out of his grasp and stormed through the front door.

"Lizzy?"

Her father came up behind her, but she kept walking, through the parlor, into the living room and out of his reach.

She refused to face him. "What are you doing here?" Her voice wobbled, and she knew if she looked at him, she'd cry.

Daddy took a deep breath. "I—I've come back." His voice wobbled worse than hers.

"Well, I can see that. I'm not blind. Why?" She was being rude, but she didn't care.

Daddy didn't seem to either. "I've missed you, Lizzy. All of you. I can't tell you how much."

"Is that why you wrote so many letters?" She used her snottiest Herta voice.

Daddy didn't reply, and she heard him drop onto the couch. She turned to face him and waited.

Daddy pulled at a loose thread and took a deep breath. Then another. He finally spoke. "I don't have an excuse. And I don't expect you to forget the last two years. If you never spoke to me again, I'd understand."

Lizzy didn't answer. Now that he was here, right here in the same room with her, all the fervent prayers she'd prayed slipped right out of her head, and she didn't know if she ever would speak to him again. But she did.

"Where have you been?"

"Chicago. I went to Chicago to look for work."

"Did you find work?"

His shoulders slumped. "No."

"So. Where ... have ... you ... been?"

"I stayed at a shelter called the Pacific Garden Mission. I did maintenance work to earn my keep."

"Why didn't you come home?"

"I was embarrassed. I—" Daddy straightened and looked her in the eye. "I'm here now, Lizzy, and I'm going to look for a job. I thought Opa might let me stay with him."

Lizzy kept her mouth shut.

"Is your grandfather—where is he? Is he all right?" Daddy's voice broke on the last word, and he took a ragged breath.

Of course he didn't know why Opa was gone. Coming back to find the house empty must have been a shock.

"Opa stroked a while back." She still wasn't sure exactly what that meant, but she knew it wasn't good. She just knew she wanted to make her father feel bad.

It worked. All the color drained out of his face. He opened his mouth to speak, but nothing came out.

Lizzy's vision blurred, and she took an angry swipe at her eyes. "He's living at our house now. He's doing better."

Daddy rubbed his forehead with one hand. "I guess I deserved that." He leaned back and rested his head on the high-backed sofa, his eyes closed.

Lizzy studied him while he wasn't looking. She didn't know how she could have mistaken him for her brother. His thick hair was mostly gray, and he was much skinnier than she remembered. He looked like a hobo, his clothes ragged and baggy. Of course, she had only met two hobos, and they were both dirty and smelly.

She gave a cautious sniff. Good. Daddy didn't smell, and his face and hands were clean.

He sat up again and opened his eyes. "Will Opa be able to come back to the farm?"

Lizzy shrugged. "I don't know. One eye droops, and he has to use a cane. It's hard for him to get around. He needs a lot of help. So he sends us kids out here to get stuff for him. He can't even walk to church, so the Schimmelpffennings pick him up every week." She kicked at the floor with the toe of her shoe. "He's pretty mad at you. Maybe he won't want to come back when he finds out you're here."

Daddy nodded. "You could very well be right ..." He caught himself before he added 'Squirt,' but the unspoken word hung in the air.

Then he asked, "How's Ginny?"

When Lizzy didn't answer, he tried again. "How are your brothers?"

Lizzy crossed her arms over her chest and studied the floor. She didn't feel like chitchatting, so she answered fast. "Frank's in the Marines, Hank has three jobs, the twins keep getting in trouble, Gene is as smart as ever, and Ginny needs help with her knuckleball pitch." She frowned. "I'm fine, too."

She was being smart-alecky and she knew it. Smart-alecky was something Mama hated, but Lizzy didn't think her mother would be upset with her right now. She looked up.

Daddy's eyes were wet. "Frank—he joined the Marines?" The air vibrated with the pain in his voice.

Lizzy had often heard Mama and Opa talking about Daddy's time in the Great War when they didn't know she was listening. Everyone said that was the start of all his problems.

"Yes. He's a good Marine. His drill instructor wrote to Mama to tell her what a good recruit he is. Everybody's real proud of him." She wanted to tell Daddy everyone thought Frank was a better soldier than he had ever been, but the haunted look on his face took all the starch out of her.

Daddy pulled a thin handkerchief out of his back pocket. He wiped his eyes and blew his nose with it. "Hank. Hank's got three jobs. Really?"

Lizzy heard the surprise in his words. Everyone thought Hank was a little lazy. Opa always said there was no chance of Hank drowning in his own sweat. The whole family was still amazed he was willing to hold down three jobs. But she wasn't going to tell Daddy that.

So she nodded. "Sure. He's changed. He's become more ... conscientious."

Daddy smiled. "Still reading the dictionary, are you?"

Lizzy blushed and shrugged.

Daddy coughed. "Sorry. The twins. What kind of trouble? How bad?"

"They tied the door shut on the school outhouse and tipped it over. Mr. Musch was inside, and he had to crawl out one of the holes."

Mr. Musch was the school principal and a stern man.

Daddy ducked his head and tried not to smile.

"Officer Mueller keeps bringing them home and giving Mama lectures on ..." Lizzy stopped herself and finally had pity on her father. She knew if she told him about the German policeman's obnoxious lectures about the boys needing a "stronga fadder figgur," his heart would break. "Lectures on keeping them in line," she finished.

"Dieter Mueller? He's back?"

Lizzy nodded.

Daddy's face looked like he'd sucked a lemon. "He tried living here twenty-some years ago, but an immigrant from Germany wasn't real welcome right after the war."

"He moved back with his family after you left," Lizzy told him. "They hired him to be the town policeman when Vernon Maas moved to Chicago. Everybody was mad about it, but he was the only person who had police experience. He makes everyone call him Officer Mueller. No one likes him."

Daddy nodded. "I can understand that. He was a mean man." His expression softened. "But anyone can change." Then he asked, "Who was the girl on the hill yesterday? Did Doorknob scare her away?"

The ugly dog had followed them into the house and was lying next to the sofa. His tail thumped, and he whined at the sound of his name.

"What kind of a name is Doorknob?"

The dog's tail thumped again.

Daddy snapped his fingers at the dog and pointed to the first door down the hall. Doorknob jumped to his feet and trotted to the door. He stood on his hind legs and balanced himself on the door jamb. He took the doorknob gently in his mouth and turned it. The door swung open. Doorknob dropped to the floor and trotted back to Daddy.

"Good boy." He scratched the head pressed into his hand. "So, who was that girl?"

"Herta Mueller, Officer Mueller's daughter. Wait a minute. You were here yesterday?"

"I slipped down to the cellar when I saw you coming. I'm sorry. But you took me by surprise. I wasn't ready to talk to anyone yet."

Lizzy wasn't sure what to say. There was an awkward pause. Finally, "Mama's sure going to be surprised to see you."

Her father didn't answer, and Lizzy didn't like his silence. "You *are* coming home with me?"

Daddy reached out to her, but Lizzy backed away. "Just answer me."

"I can't come home yet."

"Why not?"

"There are ..." He stopped and seemed to search for the right words.

Lizzy waited.

"There are problems I have to straighten out before I can come home."

"Is that what I'm supposed to tell everybody? You've got *problems?*" Suddenly she was yelling. "Everybody knows you've got problems! We've known that for years!"

"Lizzy!" Her father's voice was strong, commanding, the way she remembered.

Her mouth clamped shut in surprise.

"Please, listen to me, Squirt."

She folded her arms across her chest and waited.

"I have to take care of a few things before I can come home."

"What things?"

"I can't tell you that right now. All I can do is ..." He broke off and shook his head. "I can't believe I'm saying this. All I can do is ask you to trust me."

Lizzy stared at him.

Daddy looked at the floor, then out the window. Finally, he looked at Lizzy. "Please don't tell anyone I'm here. I'd like to wait and tell everyone myself. When the time is right."

Lizzy couldn't believe what she was hearing. Not tell anyone? How could he ask that of her? How could she not tell anyone?

Then she knew the answer. "Because when I'm gone, you're going to walk out the door and never come back, aren't you? *Aren't you?*"

Tears streaming down her face, she ran out of the room and out of the house.

# Chapter Four

She stumbled down the porch steps and kept running. She heard Daddy running behind her. He got past her and stepped in her path. She tried to get around him, but Doorknob was right beside her. She tripped over the troublesome dog and fell.

Daddy didn't try to help her up. He didn't touch her. He knelt beside her on the dirt lane. She was sobbing, and she couldn't stop.

Doorknob whined and pushed against her. She grabbed the stinky dog by the neck and buried her face in his fur. He sat perfectly still until her sobs wound down to snotty hiccups.

Daddy was still on one knee next to her in the dirt. "I'm not going anywhere, Lizzy. I promise." He took a deep breath. "What I can't promise is if your mama will want me to come home or even want me around. But I want to try to make amends for everything …"

Lizzy stood up. She didn't want to hear his excuses. "I have to get some things for Opa."

Daddy sighed. He nodded and rose to his feet. "What do you need?"

She ignored his question and walked back to the house. She went down the hall to Opa's bedroom and Daddy followed her. He watched her pull the pouch of pipe tobacco out of the drawer in the night stand. She found the bottle of tonic water in the dresser.

"Still drinking his tonic, I see."

Lizzy nodded. "It prevents malaria." She tucked the bottle in one coat pocket and put the tobacco in the other.

"Um-hmm," Daddy said with a raised eyebrow. He followed Lizzy back to the porch, and they stood there for a few moments. Lizzy didn't know what to say.

"Well, Squirt ..." Daddy caught himself. He started over. "I should be here most of the time. If I have to leave, I'll try to be back by three o'clock or so. You could come visit me after school."

Lizzy shrugged.

"Okay. Well." Daddy looked at the sun dropping close to the horizon. "You better get on home. It'll be dark before you know it."

Lizzy started down the lane. She turned around. Daddy and Doorknob were watching her. "I won't tell Mama or Opa or Ginny or the boys. For now. Bye, Doorknob."

Doorknob yipped once and his tail thumped wildly, but he stayed put. His allegiance was clear.

Lizzy trudged down the lane, never looking back. She didn't want to know if Daddy was watching her. She didn't care. Did she? The question slowed her step, and she walked to Hobbs Hill, deep in thought.

She stopped. Herta was riding a slow circle eight at the top of the hill.

What did she want now? Well, there was only one way to find out. Lizzy squared her shoulders and marched up the hill. She stepped right in the path of Herta and her new bicycle.

Herta glided around her with no problem and rode another circle. Lizzy grabbed the handlebars when she passed by again. Herta jerked out of her grasp. She lost her balance and crashed to the ground. She jumped to her feet, dusting the dirt off her bottom.

She pulled the bike up and dusted off the seat. "Watch what you're doing. This bike cost a lot of money."

"Why do you keep following me? What's your problem?"

"You're the one with the problem. My dad said he's still watching your grandfather's house, and anybody he finds there is in big trouble."

Lizzy frowned. "What's he going to do to me? Opa asked me to get his pipe tobacco." She pulled the bag out of her pocket as proof. "I have every right to be there."

Herta gave her a tight-lipped smile. "Maybe it's not you he's watching." She turned and rode away fast.

Lizzy shivered. What did that mean? Could Officer Mueller know about Daddy? Why would Officer Mueller know about Daddy? She clutched her coat around her and hurried down the road.

***

Lizzy heard Mama in the kitchen when she got home. She dropped her book bag on the hall table and ran up the stairs without taking off her coat. Mama could always tell when she'd been crying, and Lizzy wanted to rinse her face and eyes. She slipped into the bathroom and dipped a wash cloth in the water in the wash bowl. She held it to her eyes for several moments. Then she dried her face and walked downstairs to Opa's room.

She knocked on his door, and he opened it at once. He took the contraband with a smile. "Thanks, Squirt," he whispered and shut the door.

Lizzy hung her coat on the hall tree. She pulled *Great American History* out of her bag and walked down the hall to the living room in her stocking feet. She flopped onto the sofa. The radio was on, and Jimmie Davis was singing "You Are My Sunshine."

Mama walked in and flipped the knob on the Philco. The room went silent. "Why do you have the radio on when you're supposed to be doing your homework?"

"I—I just got home. The radio was already on."

Mama took a breath. "I'm sorry. I didn't mean to snap. It's just—that song hits a nerve. Your father loved it. He had it memorized before it was even a week on the radio. He always said …"

Lizzy's mouth dropped open, and Mama stopped herself. She bit her bottom lip and when she spoke, her words were soft. "You don't remember, do you?"

Lizzy's voice trembled. "Remember what?"

Mama's eyes glistened, and she shook her head. "Nothing." She was silent for several moments, then took a breath and squared her shoulders. "Nothing," she repeated firmly. "I need you to walk to Aunt Meg's and get Ginny. She went home with the girls after song practice today. It's going to be dark soon. I don't want her walking home alone." Mama pulled Lizzy to her feet. "Don't stay long. Supper is in an hour."

***

Lizzy's feet carried her down John Q Street, but her thoughts were in a thousand other places.

*What am I supposed to do? How can I keep this secret from Mama? Why did I promise Daddy I wouldn't tell…*

Lizzy stopped so quickly she almost tripped.

*I didn't promise him I wouldn't tell Elinor.*

She ran the rest of the way to her cousin's house.

Aunt Meg was in the kitchen washing dishes when Lizzy arrived. Uncle Charlie had surprised Aunt Meg with a table radio when he got a fulltime job at Caterpillar. Aunt Meg ran it all day, every day, and today Lizzy heard the surging organ music that signaled the end of *The Romance of Helen Trent*. An advertisement for Rinso soap came on, and Aunt Meg turned the volume down. She reached out and pulled Lizzy into a hug. "Hi, sweet girl."

Lizzy loved her aunt almost as much as she loved her mother, and she hugged her back hard.

Aunt Meg took Lizzy's chin in her hand. "What's wrong? You look like you've been crying."

Lizzy thought fast. "I'm reading *Anne of Green Gables* again." She was embarrassed at how easily the lie slipped out.

Aunt Meg laughed. "Oh, honey, I still cry when I read that," she admitted. "Norrie's up in her room. Did she know you were coming over?"

"No, I'm here to pick up Ginny, but I'll go talk to Elinor first, if that's okay."

"Of course. Go on upstairs."

Lizzy ran up the familiar staircase and opened Elinor's door, knocking as she walked in.

Elinor looked up from one of her brothers' *Green Hornet* comic books. She started to smile until she saw Lizzy's face. "Shut the door." When the door closed, she said, "What's wrong? Did Herta bother you again?"

Lizzy shook her head. "No. Well, yes. But that's not the problem. Not all of it." She climbed onto the bed with her cousin. She didn't know how or where to start.

She sat still for so long Elinor finally snapped her fingers in front of Lizzy's face. "What is it? You're scaring me."

"Daddy's back."

Elinor didn't blink for several seconds. Then she sputtered, "Is he—where is—what did Aunt Annie ..." She stammered to a stop.

"He's out at Opa's house, and he made me promise not to tell anyone he's back. It was his voice I heard yesterday. He's the one in the house, using the cups and saucers and stuff." Lizzy began to cry. "I promised him I wouldn't tell anyone at home he's back, but I didn't promise I wouldn't tell you. I had to tell somebody, Norrie, I just had to."

Elinor put her arms around Lizzy and patted her back. "Shhh. Someone will hear you."

Lizzy nodded and sniffed and rubbed her nose on her coat sleeve. She told Elinor the whole story between sniffles. When she finished, she dried her eyes.

"What should I do?"

Elinor's eyes were wide with shock. "I don't know."

Lizzy leaned forward. "You're not going to tell, are you?"

"No, of course not. But—do you think he's in trouble? Is he wanted by the law?"

"I don't know, but Herta followed me again, and she said her dad is still watching the house, and I told her I didn't care … and she said, 'Maybe it's not you he's watching.'"

Elinor's hand went to her mouth. "Officer Mueller knows he's there?"

Lizzy nodded. "I think so. But why does he care?" Her voice rose again, and Elinor put a cautious finger to her lips.

The two girls sat in silence for several moments. Elinor shook her head, confused. "So he's in trouble."

"I don't think so." Lizzy frowned. "I don't know. He didn't say anything about being in trouble. He said he had to take care of a few things."

"Well, if it's not trouble, why won't he tell you what things he has to take care of? Don't you think you should find out?"

Lizzy didn't have an answer, and the knot that had been growing in her stomach expanded. *Am I helping him get away with something by not telling anyone where he is? What did he mean by "take care of a few things"?*

Lizzy sighed. She would be going back to the farm tomorrow, whether she wanted to or not.

# Chapter Five

Thursday morning, Lizzy stared at the ten problems in her math book. The words seemed to float on the page, and she closed her eyes. What if Daddy was in real trouble? What would she do?

She could hear Norma Jean Gosda scribbling in the seat next to her. When the scribbling stopped, Lizzy opened her eyes. Norma Jean nodded toward the front of the room.

Mrs. Himmel stared at her with concern. "Having trouble, Lizzy?"

"No." *Not unless you count a father who could be running from the law.*

She tried to read the first story problem in her math book. Three tries later, the words still didn't make sense.

> Millie has 60 marbles in a bag. Twenty percent of the marbles are blue. How many marbles are blue?

Lizzy sighed. *Where did Millie get sixty marbles? Who cared what color they were?* She wrote down the number sixty, then the number twenty. Then she erased them both. She had no idea what to do next, so she put a question mark on her note paper and moved on to question two.

> Walter earned one dollar the week he worked for his grandfather. He gave fifteen percent of his dollar to his brother Hank when ...

Mrs. Himmel drummed her fingers on her desktop. "All right, everyone, if you finished your problems, please bring your paper to my desk. If you didn't get finished, you'll need to take them home. Put your math away, and get out your history books. Page eighty-eight." She turned and began writing questions on the blackboard.

Lizzy snapped her book shut and opened her desktop. She shoved the math book in and took out *Great American History.*

Herta came up the aisle from the back of the room. She waved her paper in Lizzy's face and reached down to pinch Lizzy's arm. Hard. Lizzy gasped.

Mrs. Himmel turned around at the sound, but Herta was already past Lizzy's desk. She set her paper down on the teacher's desk. "I'm finished, Mrs. Himmel. I just love math." She gave the teacher a big smile.

Mrs. Himmel nodded. "Thank you, Herta. Return to your desk. I want everyone to read 'Jefferson makes a Great Deal,' and look for the answers to the questions on the board. We'll discuss them after lunch." She turned back to her writing.

Herta walked past Lizzy's desk again. She reached out to flip Lizzy's history book shut. She had a bruise on her wrist, and Lizzy poked it hard with her pencil. Herta jerked back in surprise and returned to her desk.

Lizzy tried to concentrate on the history assignment, but the morning dragged. Finally, lunchtime was only five minutes away. History books slapped shut and desktops opened. Mrs. Himmel finished the questions they would discuss later that afternoon.

"Get your coats and lunch boxes," she said over her shoulder.

Twenty children rushed for the coatroom. Danny Graff pushed past Herta, then stuck out a foot to trip her. She went down with a loud thump, and everyone laughed. Herta jumped to her feet. She shoved her way through the clump of kids and grabbed her lunch box off the coatroom shelf. She saw Lizzy's box and ... the box hit the floor with a loud clang.

Lizzy picked it up without a word and went back to her desk. She set the lunch box down while she slipped on her coat. Herta strolled by and knocked it off the desk, then kicked it halfway down the aisle.

Ernie Fischer reached out and grabbed the box before it sailed past his desk. He walked it back, deliberately running into Herta's desk on his way.

"Watch it!" Herta gave Ernie a shove. "Mrs. Himmel, Ernie took Lizzy's lunch box!"

That was too much for the other children, and they all began talking at once.

"Herta knocked it off Lizzy's desk!"

"Then she kicked it down the aisle!"

"Herta's lying!"

"She's been picking on Lizzy all morning!"

Herta's face turned brick red. She crossed her arms and clamped her mouth shut.

Mrs. Himmel finished writing the last question and put the chalk down. She turned to face the class. "Quiet! You will eat your lunches here in the room, with no talking, if you don't quiet down immediately."

Silence.

Ernie handed the lunch box back to Lizzy and returned to his seat. The lunch bell sounded. No one moved.

Mrs. Himmel gave Herta a long look, and the girl's face turned a shade darker.

"Class dismissed," Mrs. Himmel said.

Herta grabbed her lunch box and charged for the door, but Mrs. Himmel's quiet voice stopped her. "Herta. Take your lunch down to the front office and wait for me there."

There was a soft sigh of satisfaction from the other students. Herta didn't turn around. She gave a quick nod and hurried out of the classroom.

Everyone else began chattering and the room emptied. Mrs. Himmel came and stood by Lizzy's desk. "Has Herta been behaving poorly?"

Lizzy nodded.

Mrs. Himmel perched on the edge of the desk, something she absolutely forbade the children to do. "I appreciate the fact you haven't tattled on Herta. I know she can be difficult. I'll have a talk with her now, but if she continues to mistreat you, please let me know, and we'll take further steps to deal with her behavior."

Lizzy wondered if "deal with" meant the same thing to Mrs. Himmel as it did to Opa.

Mrs. Himmel smiled. "You've always been a tenderhearted person, Lizzy. Please try to find it in you to be kind to Herta, even if she's unkind to you."

Lizzy blushed, remembering the pencil poke, but she nodded. Mrs. Himmel leaned over and gave her an unexpected hug. "Thank you, dear. Now, go find Elinor and eat your lunch."

Lizzy grabbed her lunch box and ran out the door.

★★★

Elinor stared at Lizzy, her mouth open. "What does she mean, be *kind* to her?"

The two girls sat alone on a pile of dry leaves under a sugar maple tree at the edge of the school yard.

Lizzy shrugged. "I don't know. How can you be kind to such a … a …" she stopped. She knew a lot of words, but she didn't know a word bad enough for Herta.

"Do you think she saw Uncle Frank yesterday?" Elinor asked.

Lizzy shook her head. "I don't think so."

Elinor took a bite of her peanut butter sandwich. "What if she keeps snooping around and finds him? What are you going to do? You know she'll tell her father."

"I don't know." Lizzy's voice sharpened. "I only know if she says or does anything to hurt my family, I'll never forgive her. And I'll make her pay."

They both looked back at the playground where the other students swarmed on and around and under the playground equipment. Herta stood on the monkey bars trying to push Ernie off the top spot. He didn't budge.

"Ernie got my lunch box after Herta knocked it off my desk."

"I think he's sweet on you." Elinor spoke in a whisper even though there was no one around to hear.

"Don't say that."

"Why not? Don't you think he's cute?"

Lizzy blushed. Ernie's coal-black hair and bright blue eyes made every girl in sixth grade swoon, but if her brothers ever got wind of the idea she liked Ernie, he would be tortured without mercy.

Ernie and Herta continued to shove and push at one another on the monkey bars, but Ernie had his feet hooked securely around the rung beneath him. No matter how hard Herta pushed or pulled, he stayed upright on the top circle.

Mr. Musch came out of the back door of the school and watched them tussling. "Herta Mueller! Ernie Fischer! My office—now!"

He pulled the rope on the school bell, and the clang sounded clearly across the school yard. Children flowed into the brick building from all directions. Herta and Ernie turned left inside the door when everyone else turned right.

Back in class, Mrs. Himmel began a short explanation of homonyms, and Lizzy's thoughts wandered.

*Why was Officer Mueller watching Opa's house? Did he know about Daddy? Was Daddy wanted for a crime? Had he hurt someone?* The thought came to Lizzy out of the blue and she gasped out loud.

"Are you all right, Lizzy?" Mrs. Himmel frowned, concern in her voice.

Lizzy took a breath and nodded. "I'm fine."

The frown remained, but Mrs. Himmel nodded. "All right. Can you give me an example of a homonym?"

Lizzy blinked rapidly. Her mind was blank.

Norma Jean raised her hand. "I have one."

Mrs. Himmel watched Lizzy for another moment. "We'll come back to you, Lizzy." She turned her attention to Norma Jean. "What's your word?"

"Cover."

"Give me two sentences using cover as a homonym."

Norma Jean nodded. "'Sally put a cover on the bed,' and 'When my grandma gets mad, we all run for cover.'"

Everyone laughed, even Mrs. Himmel, but the teacher shook her head. "I'm not sure that would be a true homonym. The meanings are very similar."

Ernie's hand shot in the air. "There's another use for the word cover."

"Yes?" said Mrs. Himmel. "Use it in a sentence."

"'When the soldier got to church, he took off his cover.'"

Most of the boys understood Ernie's sentence, but Mrs. Himmel smiled at some of the confused looks on the other students. "Can you explain that, Ernie?"

"It's the word guys in the military use for a hat or cap."

"Very good, but I'm still not sure it's a homonym. With a true homonym, the meanings are completely different. Lizzy, have you thought of a word?"

"Bat." Lizzy gave her examples quickly. "'My brothers have only one bat, so they have to share'" and 'There was a bat flying in our backyard.'"

"Very good. That's a true homonym."

Mrs. Himmel continued the lesson, and Lizzy tried hard to pay attention the rest of the afternoon. She'd have to worry about Daddy later.

But when Mr. Musch rang the bell for dismissal at 3:30, Lizzy's thoughts jumped right back to her father, who was probably waiting for her out at the farmhouse. She needed to talk to him, but how was she going to walk out there today without Ginny tagging along?

She left the classroom and walked down the hall to the front door. That's when all thoughts of a trip to the farmhouse fled. Because Frank Richter was standing in the front door of the school house.

Frank Richter, *Junior*. Cover in hand.

# Chapter Six

"Frank!"

Lizzy heard the delighted squeal and saw Ginny throw herself into her brother's arms. Frank picked Ginny up and swung her around. Marianne danced beside them, pulling at Frank's belt and begging for her own hug and a swirl.

Frank laughed and picked up his cousin with his other arm and swung them both in big circles.

Mr. Musch marched down the hall from his office. Frank saw him coming and stopped swinging. He set the girls down and turned to the principal with a sharp about-face and a snappy salute.

The stern-faced principal, a Marine himself in the Great War, returned the salute. "At ease, Marine." He allowed himself a brief smile, and he reached out to shake Frank's hand. "Please come see me sometime while you're home."

Frank nodded. "Of course, sir. You're on my list."

"Good. Carry on." Mr. Musch turned and went back to his office.

Frank stood tall and straight in his Marine service uniform. His short blond hair gleamed, his collar was crisp, and his tie was knotted just so. He was so handsome Lizzy thought she would explode with pride. She had to push through a group of gawking girls to get to her brother.

Frank saw her coming and his expression softened. "Hello, Lizzy." He gave her a gentle hug. Then he held her at arm's length, and Lizzy knew what he was going to say.

"You look more like Mama every day."

She stood taller because she knew it was a compliment. She was too big to swing, but Frank gave her another hug that lifted her off the floor, and she couldn't help but laugh.

He looked over her shoulder where several of her classmates were gathered. Lizzy followed his gaze. Ernie was at the head of the line, and Frank gave him a stern look. Ernie's ears turned bright red, but he walked to Frank and held out his hand.

"Welcome home." His voice squeaked on the word home.

Frank ignored the squeak and gave the boy's hand a firm shake. "Thank you, Ernie."

That opened the floodgates, and Frank was surrounded by a swarm of boys, all admiring his cover, his uniform, his boots, and all asking questions one on top of the other.

"How long are you home for?"

"Where are you going to be stationed?"

"What's boot camp like?"

"How does it feel to fire an M1 Garand?"

"How many push-ups can you do?" Marvin Schmidtgall, a scrawny fifth-grader who was always getting picked on by the older boys, asked the last question.

Frank smiled. "A whole lot more than I could when I left home."

Elinor came running down the hall. Frank gave her a hug, cutting off the boys' stream of questions. The four girls left the school with Frank in their midst.

"Have you been home yet?" Lizzy asked him.

Frank shook his head. "Mama met me at the bus station. She took my bag home and told me to surprise you girls. I think she's still cooking my 'welcome home' supper." He winked. "At least, I hope she is."

He turned to the others and began quizzing them about their school work and what books they were reading. Frank led all the cousins in his love for reading.

"Did you finish *Sense and Sensibility*?" he asked Elinor.

Elinor nodded. "Finally. Wouldn't you know I'm named after the practical one? Me? Practical?"

Frank smiled. "Maybe you should work on that."

Ginny grabbed Frank's hand to get his attention. "Lizzy's reading *Nancy Drew* to me every night."

"Not *Pride and Prejudice*?"

Lizzy grinned and shook her head. She had been named for a character from that book, but she had never been able to get through it. "Nancy Drew's a lot more exciting than Lizzy Barrett."

"Bennet." Frank and Elinor both corrected her.

They reached John Q, and Elinor leaned over and whispered something in Marianne's ear. The little girl's face lit up, and she turned to Frank.

"Does anybody at our house know you're home?"

He shook his head. "I don't think so. Why don't you go tell them?"

Marianne took off running. Elinor tried to keep up with her, but she had to stop to pick up the papers floating out of Marianne's bouncing book bag.

Lizzy and Ginny walked on either side of Frank. Ginny hung onto his hand, swinging his arm back and forth as she skipped. "Me and Marianne are going to build a treehouse in their back yard."

"Marianne and I," Frank corrected, but she was too busy talking to notice.

"Mr. Thompson is my teacher this year. He said he spanked you once. Is that true?"

"Maybe." Frank grinned at her. "I better not hear of you getting any spankings."

"Mama says I'm Mr. Thompson's pet, so I'll be okay. But the twins are getting in lots of trouble."

"What kind of trouble?"

"They tied Mr. Musch in the privy and tipped it over." When she added, "He had to crawl out the hole," Frank laughed out loud.

Ginny moved on to a new topic. "Hertie-Gertie is being a real snot, especially to Lizzy, and Lizzy won't even tattle on her. Somebody needs to give Herta a spanking, even if her father is the police officer."

Frank glanced at Lizzy. She didn't want to complain about Herta. She felt shy with Frank. He looked so different. So grown up. He kept smiling down at her, and she smiled back, but she didn't know what to say.

Ginny pulled on Frank's hand. "I've been playing softball with the neighbors—wait 'til you see my knuckleball pitch."

Frank suppressed a grin. "You've got a knuckleball?"

Ginny sighed. "It needs some work."

"I'll help you with that." Frank squeezed her hand, and Ginny gave a happy skip.

"Okay, Squeaker," he continued, "how about you give Lizzy a chance to say something?"

"Lizzy doesn't like to talk. I love to talk. You don't mind, do you Lizzy?"

"I mind." Frank gave Ginny's nose a tweak. "I want to hear about this essay she got published in the paper."

"It's all about you—" Ginny started, but Frank covered her mouth with a gentle hand.

"I want Lizzy to tell me."

Lizzy stared at the ground as she talked. "The newspaper asked everyone in the sixth grade class to submit an essay about someone from Black Hawk Grove they admire, so I wrote about you." She risked a quick glance at Frank. He was staring straight ahead with a strange look on his face.

"I used some of the stories you sent in your letters. I hope you don't mind."

It took a second for Frank to answer. "I don't mind at all."

Ginny broke her silence. "Lizzy won first place. The editor said her essay was the most interesting, *and* the best written."

Lizzy gave her a startled glance.

"I read the letter he sent you." Ginny turned back to Frank. "He even told Mama he thought she had the ... the ..."

"Potential?" Frank suggested.

"Yep. The potential to be a phemona—phenonum—phemonamal ..."

Frank stifled another grin, and Lizzy murmured, "Phenomenal?"

"Yeah, that's it. I don't know what that word means, but I think he was saying you're gonna be a good writer."

Frank smiled at Lizzy. "She already is." He gave her a gentle nudge. "I'm proud of you, Squirt. I can't wait to read it."

Lizzy didn't know what to say, but she was spared by the loud bang of their front door. The twins and Gene burst out of the house and ran up the street to greet their older brother.

Frank smacked both the twins on the back of their heads before he gave them each a bear hug. "What's wrong with you two, tying Mr. Musch in the privy and tipping it over?"

Joe and Jack talked over one another to tell Frank how they'd planned the whole thing.

"You would have been impressed!" Jack exclaimed. "Everything went perfect. Of course, we took all the heat, even though ..." he stopped.

Frank tried to frown. "Even though what?" He looked at Gene, then Lizzy. Everyone except Ginny had been in on the dastardly deed. Hank had provided the rope they used, and Gene had been their lookout. Lizzy knew what they were doing and didn't tattle on them, which the twins considered involvement, for a girl.

Frank shook his head. "Don't go sucking the rest of the family into your trouble-making," he said, his voice light. He turned to Gene and pulled him into a hug.

"Look at you, little brother. You're as tall as the twins."

That brought shouts of protest from Joe and Jack. They walked the rest of the block trying to stretch up over Gene to prove they were taller, though Gene had almost caught up with them in the three months Frank had been gone.

Mama and Opa were waiting for them on the front porch. Opa reached into the group to pull Frank into the house. "Give the man room to breathe."

Everyone trooped inside. Frank's boots hit the rug first, and a tumble of shoes piled up next to them. Lizzy could smell the cinnamon in a fresh batch of snickerdoodles, Frank's favorite cookie, coming from the kitchen.

"Did you know Frank would be home today?" Ginny asked Mama.

"Yes, I knew, but I wanted to surprise all of you. I didn't want to take the chance he'd be delayed, and you'd be disappointed."

"Where's Hank?" Frank glanced eagerly down the hall.

"He's got a new job," Mama told him. "The Pfeiffers have him cleaning out their brooder houses. They started him out harvesting and butchering, but ..." She laughed. "The first time he tried to wring a chicken's neck, he just strangled the poor thing. He finally dropped it, and he said it wobbled around the yard for a few seconds, then toppled over."

Everyone had heard the story more than once, but they still enjoyed it. Frank's laughter filled the hall, and everyone laughed with him.

"Hank felt so bad, he said he'd rather dig through muck than choke another chicken."

Frank laughed harder. "I'm not going to let him live that one down!"

There was no limit when the two oldest boys teased one another, and Lizzy missed the once-constant banter between them. They were thick as thieves, Opa always said, and she knew Hank had been the loneliest without Frank.

Frank took off his cover and hung it carefully on the hall tree. Lizzy and Ginny tossed their book bags on the hall table. Mama didn't even suggest they start their homework. They filed into the dining room, with Opa leading the way.

Opa gave Frank the chair at the head of the table and everyone else took their regular seats. Mama set the snickerdoodles in the center of the table and poured Frank a cup of coffee.

Joe grabbed three cookies. "What's your drill sergeant like?"

"He's tough. Got quite a mouth on him. I've learned words I never heard before." Frank grinned at Mama as he said it.

"Don't think of using them here," she warned him.

Frank winked. "Wouldn't dream of it."

"Have your bunkmate's eyebrows grown back?" Ginny giggled as she asked the question, and Frank laughed with her.

"Not even close."

The boys had a million more questions, and Frank answered them all. The talk of guns, battle techniques, and squad formations went over Lizzy's head, but she could have listened to Frank talk all day.

Ginny got tired of being ignored. She slipped out of her chair and onto Frank's lap. He settled her with a smile and a kiss on top of her head. No one said anything, and maybe no one else remembered, but Lizzy did. Daddy used to do the same thing with both his girls.

Ginny leaned back and rested her head on his shoulder. "How long can you stay?"

"Oh, about a week."

"Only a week? But that's not long enough!"

Lizzy sighed. They would be in school the whole time Frank was home.

Ginny's thoughts were going the same direction. She turned to her mother. "Can we stay home from school tomorrow?"

All the boys shouted with laughter, and Mama looked at her youngest child. "What do you think, young lady?"

Ginny slumped back against her brother with a dramatic sigh. "I won't learn a thing."

There were footsteps on the front porch, and the room got silent. The front door opened, and they heard Hank come in and slip out of his shoes.

Frank slid Ginny off his lap and stood up. Suddenly, there was a loud cry, and Hank pounded down the hall to the dining room. He burst through the swinging door, and Frank met him half-way around the table.

The two brothers hugged fiercely and slapped one another on the back. All the other children were talking at the same time, but no one seemed to mind the noise. Lizzy saw Mama wipe her eyes, and even Opa had a smile on his face. Today, all was right with the world. Frank was home!

# Chapter Seven

"Roast beef for supper?" Frank pulled out his regular chair with a loud scrape. "Man, am I glad I'm home."

Mama sat a large bowl of potatoes and carrots next to the roast beef. "Engle Ben gave me that roast as a welcome home gift for you. Be sure and stop by the Golden Rule tomorrow to tell him thank you."

"Yes, ma'am." Frank took a big chunk of the meat and piled a large helping of vegetables next to it. "I haven't seen a meal like this for three months."

Opa took the bowl of vegetables from his grandson. "Then you should be the one to lead the blessing."

Frank laughed. "Yes, sir. Sorry. I got excited." He bowed his head, and the others followed.

"Come Lord Jesus, be our guest, and let these gifts to us be blessed. Amen."

The 'amen' was hardly out before Joe grabbed the plate of meat, and Jack tried to take it from him. Mama slapped both their hands. She handed the plate to Hank.

Frank took a bite of roast and watched the twins bicker. He chewed and swallowed. "So, what other trouble have you two been getting into? I mean, other than tipping over outhouses." He took another bite of roast and waited.

There was an awkward silence. Neither twin answered.

Frank finished chewing and spoke again. "Dieter Mueller stopped me outside the school this afternoon. He wanted to know why I was back in town. Told him I was on leave before my first deployment.

"Then he said something I wasn't expecting," Frank continued. "He said he thought maybe I was here because I'd heard of some serious trouble in the Richter family. Told him I didn't know what he was talking about." He paused. "Can either of you tell me what he meant?"

Joe pushed his carrots around his plate, and Jack swirled a finger around the rim of his water glass.

Opa slammed his fork down, and his voice thundered across the table. "You two won't tell him, I will. Mueller keeps bringin' 'em home in the police car. Once he caught 'em eggin' the Fornoffs' house. Once they were tryin' to break into the soda machine at the gas station after hours. And once, they were sneakin' into the warehouse at the lumber yard. Don't know what *that* was about."

Frank placed his fork on his plate and leaned forward. He tapped the table in front of Joe. "Hey."

Joe looked up first, then Jack. Both were pale. Joe chewed on his thumbnail, and Jack's heel tapped a staccato beat under the table.

"You two going to keep up that behavior, or are you going to stop? You're disrespecting God, and you're disrespecting Mama."

Joe spoke first. "We'll stop. I promise."

Jack nodded his head in agreement. "We'll stop."

"Good." Frank held their gaze for another moment, then gave a brief nod toward their mother.

The twins spoke in unison. "We're sorry, Mama."

Mama nodded. "Thank you." She studied the two boys, her expression kind but firm. "A good first step would be to apologize to the Fornoffs."

Both boys nodded.

Opa was still frowning. "And you can respect your mama by doing your homework without complaining, for once."

Joe opened his mouth to protest, but Opa stopped him. "I know you have homework."

Joe drooped. "Okay."

"That goes for all of you." Mama passed the vegetable bowl to Lizzy. "No games or radio for anyone until all homework is done. Did you get your spelling words written, Ginny? What about your math problems, Lizzy?"

Lizzy sighed. She plopped a helping of carrots on her plate and passed the bowl to Gene.

He nudged her and spoke under his breath. "I'll do them for you."

Lizzy slipped a few of her carrots onto his plate as a silent thank-you.

After supper, Mama, Frank, and Hank did dishes while the other children did their homework. The twins pretended to read *Gulliver's Travels*. Opa helped Ginny with her spelling words, and Lizzy recopied the work for the math problems Gene slipped to her when Opa wasn't looking.

When Mama and the older boys were finished with dishes, everyone else was already settled on the living room floor, ready to play Monopoly and listen to "The Green Hornet." Ginny didn't understand the game and soon lost all her money. Gene eventually bought so many properties the twins got disgusted and quit. Little brother stacked his money with a satisfied smile.

Ginny scooted close to Frank and leaned her head on his shoulder. He put an arm around her, and she promptly fell asleep. He lifted her to the sofa, and while she snored, Frank told them all about his first assignment for the Marines.

"I'll be headed to Hawaii sometime next month. I've been assigned to guard duty on the *Arizona*. It's a battleship stationed with the rest of our Pacific fleet at Pearl Harbor."

"Where's Hawaii?" Joe asked him.

"It's in the Pacific Ocean, west of California."

Opa stumped down the hall to his room and came back with the globe that was one of his prized possessions. He placed it on the floor in the middle of the children. Frank spun it around to show them the tiny string of islands he would call home for the next year.

Lizzy couldn't speak when she saw how far Hawaii was from Illinois. *Frank's going to be awfully far away. For a whole year.*

Jack spun the globe and his finger landed on another, much larger blob of land. "Where do you think they'll send you when America gets in the war? Europe?"

"I'll probably stay on the ship in Hawaii," Frank answered. "The battleships will be the first to be deployed."

Then he looked at Mama's face. "But we're not at war, and we don't know if or when that will happen." He kept his tone light, but Mama wasn't fooled.

"We've got better things to talk about than war," she said. "You've got a full day ahead of you tomorrow," she told Frank. "There are lots of folks who want to see you besides Engle Ben."

Frank grinned. "If I wear my uniform, we might get another roast out of him."

Mama tried to suppress a smile. "Behave yourself. That roast was a generous gift. I don't want him to think we expect anything more."

Jack's eyes lit up. "Go by Tommy DeSutter's instead. He always tells Mama you were the best worker he ever had. And he's got a whole chicken coop full of fryers. Bet

58

he'd be willing to give you a couple of his best ones." Fried chicken was Jack's favorite food.

Joe, on the other hand, had a sweet tooth. "Stop at the bakery before you come home. Lorraine Priddy works there full time now. She'll be glad to send you home with fresh donuts."

Frank winced, and the sour lemon look on his face sent his brothers into peals of laughter. Lorraine had been sweet on Frank for as long as Lizzy could remember, but she had buck teeth and one eye wandered.

"You're going to have to make do with Mama's snickerdoodles," was all he said.

The night ended with more suggestions for Frank's trip around town the next day. Even Mama laughed when Gene said he could use some dirt from Talbot's dirt farm for his diorama for history class.

Lizzy nudged Ginny awake, and the two girls trudged up the stairs to bed. Lizzy turned over and stared out the window at the sliver of moon that peeked out from behind the neighbor's trees. She couldn't get Frank's words out of her mind. "… maybe I was here because I'd heard of some serious trouble in the Richter family."

*What if Mueller wasn't talking about the twins? What if he was talking about Daddy? What should I do? Should I tell Frank Daddy's home? Should I tell Daddy Frank is home? How did everything get so complicated so fast?*

She drifted off to sleep, but her dreams were troubled with images of Frank fighting someone. She could never see if he was fighting a Nazi—or Daddy.

# Chapter Eight

Friday stretched into the longest day of the year. Mrs. Himmel frowned when she saw Lizzy's sloppy math work. The numbers were barely legible, two of the problems were wrong, and Lizzy debated telling her brother. *Even Gene gets distracted sometimes.*

At recess, Lizzy found herself alone in the cloak room with Herta. When the other girl reached for her coat, Lizzy noticed the bruise on her wrist had deepened in color, and there was another on her forearm.

*Where did those bruises come from?*

Lizzy's unasked question must have shown in her eyes, because Herta frowned and fumbled with her coat. "Stop staring at me."

Ernie came in the room behind Lizzy and reached around her to pull his jacket off one of the coat hooks. He glanced at Herta and pointed at the bruises. "What happened? Did you fall off your bike again?"

"Shut up." She pulled on her coat and pushed past Lizzy with an unnecessary shove.

Herta kept to herself for the rest of the day. While everyone else asked Lizzy questions about Frank, Herta said nothing. Her silence made Lizzy nervous. Did she know something, or did she just think she knew something? After Lizzy sharpened her pencil, she returned to her desk and caught Herta staring at her. There was such suspicion in her eyes Lizzy shivered, although she didn't know why.

The day dragged on until 2:45, when Mr. Musch came out of his office and rang the bell. Lizzy left class and met Ginny at the front door. Ginny's shoulders drooped.

"I thought Frank would be here again."

"Frank has lots of people to see," Lizzy said. "Be glad we get him to ourselves at night."

Ginny's face brightened at the thought. "He said he'd help me with my knuckleball pitch." She glanced down the hall. "Where're Elinor and Marianne?"

"They have their first tap lesson with Helen Schlicker tonight."

"I wish I could take tap lessons."

"You do know tap means tap *dancing*, right?"

"Oh." Ginny's nose wrinkled and she shuddered. "Forget that." Any kind of dancing was too girly for Ginny.

The two sisters left the school and reached Paw-Paw Street. Ginny skipped ahead of Lizzy, eager to get to the Worners' house to pet Spud and Two-Spot, her favorite dogs in the whole town.

Lizzy heard the sound of rubber on concrete before she felt the rush of air. Herta flashed by on her shiny red bike, so close Lizzy stumbled off the sidewalk when Herta grazed her arm.

Ginny had reached the Worners' house. She was reaching through a broken slat of the rickety fence that kept the dogs corralled in the dry dirt and weeds the Worners called a front yard.

Herta stood up to pedal past Ginny, but she slowed down long enough to reach out and grab the school bag on Ginny's shoulder. She jerked the strap and Ginny tumbled to the ground.

The little girl hit hard and the bag split open. Spud and Two-Spot set up a racket of frenzied barking. Books spilled out and papers flew into the air. Herta kept riding. The two dogs tried to chase her, but the fence did its job, and the little mongrels barked and jumped up and down in the corner of the yard like two noisy brown balls.

Lizzy ran down the sidewalk to her sister. Ginny was on her knees. She had her speller in one hand and her math book in the other.

Lizzy picked up the reader that lay in the grass. She reached out and took the other books from her sister. "I'll put them in my bag. You okay?"

Ginny nodded, blinking hard. "Hertie-Gertie is a stinker, and I hate her."

Lizzy knew she should probably give Ginny their mother's "We don't hate people, we hate what they do" lecture, but right now she was so mad at Herta she wanted to spit. She kept her mouth shut and helped Ginny to her feet.

Spud and Two-Spot trotted back to the girls, and Two-Spot poked his head through the broken slat. Ginny scratched his big spot first, then his little spot. The dog closed his eyes in ecstasy until Ginny gently pushed his head back through the fence.

The girls were silent as they walked down the sidewalk. They picked up Ginny's stray papers on the way.

Ginny held one out for Lizzy to see. "Look. I got a B on my spelling test. I thought Mama might put it on the bulletin board, but now ..." Her voice trailed off. The paper was torn, and the B was smudged.

"Herta's going to buy you a new bag." Lizzy stuffed Ginny's torn bag and the rest of the stray papers into her own bag. Then she grabbed Ginny's hand and pulled her down the street. Ginny had to trot to keep up, but she knew better than to protest.

Instead of going home, Lizzy kept walking. She pulled Ginny up Paw-Paw Street, past their house, and down William. They walked another two blocks to Herta's house.

Herta's bicycle was leaning against the porch, and the hateful girl sat on the top step, drinking from a newly opened bottle of Coca-Cola.

Lizzy's mouth watered. She loved Coca-Cola, but she seldom had a nickel to buy one.

Herta swiped her hand across her mouth when she saw them. The frown on her face crinkled her eyes into little slits. "What are you doing here?"

"You ruined Ginny's bag and—"

"Prove it." Herta took another swallow of soda.

"—and now she needs a new one and you're going to buy it."

"I don't know what you're talking about. I didn't do anything."

"Miss Waldmeier saw you." Lizzy didn't know if that was true or not, but Miss Waldmeier lived next door to the Worners, and the old woman kept vigilant guard of the street in a rocking chair by her front window.

Herta's frown deepened. "I don't believe you."

"I don't care if you believe me. Frank is home and when I tell him what you did, he'll come talk to your father."

Herta's top lip curled. "So? My father was a lance corporal in the German Imperial Army. He won't care what some puny Marine has to say."

Ginny had a rock in her hand before Lizzy could stop her, and Herta bolted off the step. Ginny had a good eye and a wicked throw. The rock bounced off the Muellers' front door as it slammed shut behind Herta.

Ginny picked up a second rock and was ready to pitch it after the first when a gentle hand and a quiet voice stopped her.

"Was that your knuckleball?" Hank pried the rock from Ginny's grasp. He squatted next to his sister and held the rock up for inspection. "This is a nice piece of quartz. Crack it open with a hammer and it'll be all pink and sparkly on the inside." He grinned. "Don't waste it on Herta."

Ginny had to work hard not to grin back. "I woulda hit her. The big fat chicken ran inside."

Hank laughed and stood up. He looked at Lizzy. "What are you two doing here?"

Lizzy showed him Ginny's school bag and told him what had happened. Hank examined the bag and his smile faded. He turned Ginny in a slow circle and looked her over. "You all right, Squeaker?"

Ginny shrugged. "I guess."

The Mueller's front door banged open, and Officer Mueller filled the door frame. He was wearing his uniform and hat. He stepped onto the porch, pulling a reluctant Herta with him.

"What is going on here?" Officer Mueller's booming voice made several starlings in the oak tree in his front yard flap away with loud chirps of protest.

Herta tried to pull out of her father's grasp. He tightened his hold and shook her arm. Hard.

Hank folded the torn school bag in half and turned to the girls. "Go on home. I'll take care of this."

"I said, what is going on?" Officer Mueller's voice went up a decibel and his face got red. He wasn't used to being ignored.

Hank was still facing the girls, but he raised one hand and said, "Hang on," over his shoulder.

Lizzy heard Mueller growl under his breath. Hank heard him as well, but he only smiled. "Go on. I'll be home before you know it."

Lizzy took Ginny by the hand, and they walked back the way they had come.

"We can't leave him all by himself." Ginny spoke under her breath when they were a safe distance away.

"He'll be fine." Lizzy gave an uneasy glance over her shoulder.

Herta was watching them. Officer Mueller still had a fierce grip on his daughter's arm, and there was pain on Herta's face. Her eyes met Lizzy's, and for a brief moment Lizzy saw fear in the other girl's expression. She felt an unexpected stab of sympathy. She had never seen Herta afraid of anything. She couldn't imagine being afraid of her own father.

The next instant Herta's lip lifted in a sneer. The words "some puny Marine" echoed in Lizzy's head, and her sympathy vanished.

## Chapter Nine

Lizzy scuffed the sidewalk with each step, her pace slow and deliberate. She let Ginny stop and pet the Schumm's wiener dog, examine a fallen bird nest, and read the set of initials newly carved into the massive oak on the corner of Andrew and Paw Paw.

*What is taking Hank so long? Is he talking with Officer Mueller about something besides the back pack? Maybe about Opa's house?*

She glanced over her shoulder, but there was no Hank in sight.

Ginny turned around and walked backwards in front of her. "What was Hank doing at the Muellers' house?"

"He wasn't at the Muellers' house. He was probably visiting Jane."

Hank was sweet on Jane Reinken, who lived two doors down from the Muellers. Jane was about the prettiest girl in Black Hawk Grove, and Lizzy knew there were lots of boys chasing after her, but for some reason she seemed to like Hank. Lizzy tried to see her brother the way an older girl might, but it was impossible. He was just Hank. Kind of cute and really funny, but was that enough to fool a girl like Jane?

Ginny interrupted her thoughts. "What's a lance corporal?"

"I don't know."

"What's the Interior German Army?"

"*Imperial* German Army," Lizzy corrected her. "I think they're just dumb Nazi krauts."

"Is kraut a bad word? I thought it was another word for cabbage."

"It is." Lizzy shrugged. "It's not a bad word, I guess— it's just an insult."

"But why?"

"Most Germans eat sauerkraut, so some people like to insult us by calling us krauts."

Ginny wrinkled her nose, confusion clear in her expression. "Wait a minute. Joe loves sauerkraut. So do you. If you like sauerkraut, why would it be an insult? And why would you use it to insult someone else?"

Lizzy felt her face get hot. Sometimes Ginny made too much sense for a nine-year-old. "You're right. I was just repeating what I heard. I probably shouldn't do that, should I?"

"No." Satisfied with Lizzy's admission, Ginny turned around and walked straight again. When they reached the corner of their yard, she ran ahead and raced up the porch steps.

"Take your shoes off," Lizzy called, but the little girl ran inside without stopping.

Lizzy trudged up the steps. She took off her shoes and left them on the rug inside the front door.

Ginny hopped back down the hall on her left foot, trying to untie the shoe on her right. "Fred Wistehuff and Tommy DeSutter both ordered cinnamon rolls."

Lizzy tossed her book bag on the hall table and ran for the kitchen. If the twins came home and got to the scrap rolls first, they would disappear in a heartbeat.

Ginny raced by in her stocking feet. "Hurry. The twins are coming up the back alley."

Both girls made it to the kitchen seconds before the back door slammed open. Mama was at the counter, icing a plate of perfectly shaped rolls, but she nodded toward the table. The end pieces she cut off each log of dough were cooked and on another plate, with a small amount of icing dribbled over them.

Lizzie and Ginny both had a roll in hand when the twins entered the kitchen. Joe pulled three lumps off the scrap plate and handed the last three to Jack. Opa thumped through the kitchen door in time to see Joe stuff a whole roll into his mouth. Opa pounded the floor at Joe's feet with his cane, and Joe danced away as he chewed.

"What's the matter with you?" Opa reached out and took Joe's last roll and one from Jack. Joe tried to protest, but his mouth was so full he had to swallow first. By that time, Opa had both of the confiscated rolls on a smaller plate, and he took a seat at the table.

He pointed his cane at a chair. "Get a plate, sit down, and eat like civilized human beings."

Lizzy glanced out the back door. The Schimmelpfennings' brand new, blue DeSoto sedan pulled up the alley and stopped behind the house. Gene hopped out of the passenger's side, and the car rolled away.

Gene came through the back door to the kitchen, and he groaned when he saw what everyone was eating. "Are there any left?"

Opa gave him one of his rolls, and Gene accepted it with a grateful smile. "Thanks."

Opa nodded. "Otto's driving the new car now?"

"Oscar's teaching him."

Opa studied his youngest grandson. "Driving a car's a big responsibility. Anybody gets behind the wheel of a car, they need to think long and hard about what they're doing."

"Mmm." Gene kept his eyes on his roll.

Lizzy knew Oscar was teaching Otto *and* Gene how to drive. It sounded like Opa knew, too.

She nibbled on her sweet roll, trying to make the rare treat last as long as possible. Then she set her half-eaten roll on her plate and sighed.

"Can I have that?" Joe reached across the table.

"No!" Lizzy smacked his hand. "There'd be none left for Hank."

Ginny set her roll down. "What about Frank? He won't get any either."

"Don't worry about your brothers." Mama swirled frosting on the next roll on the good plate.

"Why is Hank late getting home from work?" Opa pulled a checkered handkerchief from his pocket and wiped his mouth.

"He's late because of us," Ginny said.

Mama stopped icing and turned around. "Why?"

Ginny took a deep breath. "Herta chased me down on her new bike and grabbed my book bag and tore it, and I fell down and Spud and Two-Spot wanted to chase her, but they couldn't get out of their yard, and my spelling paper got torn, and—I got a B, Mama—and Lizzy went after her and Herta wouldn't admit what she'd done, so ... so ..."

Ginny stopped. Mama had strictly forbidden her to throw rocks at anyone. Before she could tell the rest of the story, Joe asked, "How big a rock did you use?"

Ginny didn't reply.

"Did you hit her?"

"No."

Mama sighed and shook her head. "Ginny, stand up and turn around."

Ginny stood and turned, expecting a swat. She stayed just out of reach of her mother.

Mama glanced at the back of her dress. "I'll have to mend that tonight."

Ginny looked over her shoulder and turned in a complete circle, trying to see the back of her dress. There was a slight tear in the skirt where she had landed on her bottom.

She slumped back in her chair. Her lips were pressed into a hard pout, and her red face betrayed her anger over the torn dress. "Hertie-Gertie's a stinkpot."

Mama pointed the frosting knife at her youngest daughter. "Her name is Herta, and we don't call anyone a stinkpot. You don't have to like her, but you do have to treat her with respect. The way you would want to be treated. Matthew 7:12."

Ginny stayed slumped in her chair.

"Genevieve Rose. Matthew 7:12."

At the use of her full name, Ginny rolled her eyes, but she straightened up and repeated the verse. "'Therefore, all things whatsoever ye would that men should do to you, do ye even so to them: for this is the law and the prophets.'"

"Thank you."

Lizzy waited a few seconds, then picked up the story where Ginny had left off. "Hank came by, and we told him what happened. He sent us home and said he'd take care of it. He was talking to Officer Mueller when we left."

"I tink Herta needs a stronga fadder figur." Joe spoke in a perfect imitation of Officer Mueller's heavy accent.

Jack snickered, and Opa smacked the back of his head.

Hank came through the back door and saw the plates. "Oh, man, I missed the rolls, didn't I?"

Lizzy spoke. "You can have the rest of mine."

Mama opened a cupboard door and pulled out a plate with several more scrap rolls on it. "I thought you might be late." She handed the rolls to Hank. "Leave some for Frank. How's Jane?"

"She wasn't home."

"What did Officer Mueller say?" Lizzy asked.

Hank pulled a quarter out of his pocket. "This should buy Ginny another bag. I'll pick one up at work tomorrow." One of Hank's jobs was stocking shelves at Jenkins' Dry Goods.

Lizzy swallowed the last bite of her sweet roll. "I hope Herta gets a good whipping. She deserves it."

"What Herta deserves is none of your business." Mama crooked a finger at Ginny. "Come on, let's go fix your dress right now. I do wash tomorrow." She and Ginny left the kitchen.

Hank's expression was troubled. "You might want to …" He stopped and blew out a long breath. "You might want to go easy on Herta."

"Go easy? What do you mean, go easy?"

Hank thought before he answered. "If Herta's mean, it's probably because she doesn't know any better." He bit into his roll and spoke with his mouth full. "You know better. You should act like it. Weren't you listening in church last Sunday? 'Be ye kind one to another, tenderhearted, forgiving one another, even as God for Christ's sake hath forgiven you.'"

Lizzy wrinkled her nose and stuck out her tongue at her brother. Hank was Mama's son when it came to memorizing Scripture, and he often quoted Bible verses at the worst times. This was one of them.

"Then there's 'Love your enemies, and do good to them which hate you.'" Now Hank was baiting her.

Lizzy bit. "I don't want to forgive her *or* love her *or* do good to her. She goes to church, too. She never listens. Why should I?"

Hank reached out and tugged on one of Lizzy's braids. "I told you. Because you know better."

Lizzy pushed his hand away. First Mrs. Himmel asked her to be kind to Herta. Now Hank wanted her to go easy on the stuck-up girl, to forgive her. To love her. That wasn't going to happen. Didn't they know what Herta was like?

"She doesn't deserve to be forgiven."

Hank stared at her. "Are you serious? None of us deserves forgiveness. You know that." He stopped and softened his tone. "Sorry. I know she's been a real beast to you. I just don't think she knows any better. *You do.*"

Hank finished his second roll in another bite and took his plate to the sink. He winked at Lizzy. "Your turn to wash up."

Joe and Jack pushed back from the table and hurried out of the room before Lizzy could recruit one of them to help. Opa grabbed his cane, and Hank held the door for him.

Gene was the only brother left in the kitchen. "I'll help you, Lizard."

"Thanks."

Lizzy washed and Gene dried. Neither spoke until the last plate had been put away. Gene handed her the towel to dry her hands.

Lizzy took it with a frustrated sigh. "I don't care if I do know better. I still wish Ginny had hit her with that rock."

## Chapter Ten

Lizzy was up early on Saturday morning. It was her job to deliver Mama's baked goods, and she always got an early start. Her first stop was Fred Wistehuff's house.

"Boy, those cinnamon rolls sure smell good." The elderly farmer's hand shook when he took the full plate from Lizzy. She held her breath until he set the plate on the counter by the back door. He picked up the clean plate from last week's delivery and it slipped from his hand. She caught it before it hit the ground. She set it in her wagon and handed him a loaf of bread wrapped in a clean tea towel.

"Thank you much, little lady." He dropped several coins into Lizzy's hand. "You plan on going to that new picture show today?"

Lizzy nodded. "I hope so."

"Well, here you go. Maybe this will help." He dropped three more pennies in her hand.

Lizzy grinned. "Thanks, Mr. Wistehuff!"

Three hours later, her wagon was full of clean plates and empty of bread and rolls. Nine pennies in tip money in her coat pocket jingled cheerfully. The morning had been a good one. Counting the nickel Mama would give her for delivering, and the money she had saved, she would have enough for the movie.

The bright sun warmed the November morning, so Lizzy took her time walking home. She saw a faint cloud of dust at the edge of Black Hawk Grove. Her stomach sank when the cloud turned into a girl on a red bike. What was Herta doing now?

The other girl slowed as she drew closer. Lizzy ignored her. Herta began riding in circles around Lizzy and her wagon, edging closer with each pass.

Finally Herta braked directly in front of Lizzy and forced her to stop. "I want my quarter back."

"I don't have your quarter."

"You can get it."

"No, I can't."

"I need my quarter!" Herta's voice trembled, and Lizzy didn't know why.

She thought back to the fear on Herta's face and Officer Mueller's grip on her arm. "Is your dad angry about you losing a quarter?" Lizzy's voice was soft.

Herta's eyes glistened, and she gave a stubborn shake of her head. "Don't feel sorry for—he doesn't mean—I just have to—stop it!" Her eyes squinched back into mean slits and she grabbed Lizzy's arm. "I want my quarter back."

Lizzy pulled free. "It's too late. You ruined Ginny's bag. Hank was going to buy her a new one at work today, so the money's already gone."

Herta shoved her face inches from Lizzy's. "I know you've got money with you. I watched you making your deliveries this morning. Where is it?"

She grabbed Lizzy's arm again and pinned it behind her, reaching into her coat pocket at the same time. Fortunately she got the wrong pocket, and Lizzy twisted out of her grip before Herta could examine the other one.

Herta tried to grab her again, but Lizzy shoved her back. Herta yelled in her face, "I want my money back, you sissy tattle-tale—"

Suddenly Herta flipped her bike around and pedaled furiously down the road, back towards town.

A black blur raced by Lizzy, and Doorknob caught up to Herta with a ferocious bark. Herta pedaled harder and pulled ahead, but Doorknob stayed with her.

Lizzy ran, and the wagon bounced behind her, the plates clattering. She didn't want to break anything, but she wanted to get home before Doorknob gave up. *Why isn't he with Daddy?*

She didn't stop running until she got to her own street. She looked up and down Paw-Paw, certain she would find Herta lurking somewhere nearby, but there was no sign of the other girl. No Doorknob either.

She reached home, pulled the wagon around back, and went in the house through the back door. She went straight to the breadbox to get the nickel Mama always left underneath.

Opa was drinking coffee at the kitchen table. "Where you been? Didn't think you took this long to make those deliveries. Elinor's already been here looking for you." He paused. "You got enough money for the picture show this afternoon?"

Lizzy nodded. "Everybody was real pleased today. Mama's cinnamon rolls and bread always smell good. Makes people generous."

Opa reached in a pocket and pulled out a nickel. "Well, here. Take this anyway. I didn't say thank you for going out to the house for me. Buy you some of those new M&M things when you get to the movie."

Lizzy took the nickel. She didn't know what to say. Her grandfather was known to squeeze a penny until it bled. Giving up a nickel was unheard of.

"Don't go telling anybody. I ain't gonna make a habit of that."

Lizzy nodded. "Okay. Thanks."

Opa looked closely at her. "What's the matter? Who licked the red off your candy?"

Lizzy bit her lip to keep from blurting out her latest encounter with Herta. "Sissy tattle-tale" wasn't a name she wanted to stick. If she told someone every time Herta acted like a jerk, Herta would make sure the label stuck. So, Lizzy shook her head.

"I'm fine, Opa."

She knew he didn't believe her, but he didn't push.

Instead, he pulled out his pocket watch and checked the time. "Well, you better get movin'. The first showing is at 12:30. You got about half an hour if you plan to go."

Lizzy gave him an unexpected kiss on the cheek, and he harrumphed loudly. "Go on, get outta here."

"Tell Mama I'll be home to help with supper!"

Lizzy ran upstairs to get the rest of her money from her piggy bank. She slipped the coins in her coat pocket, then thought again. In case Herta had more nerve than Lizzy gave her credit for, she tied the money in her handkerchief and put the handkerchief in the hole inside her coat, where the lining had ripped away from the wool.

She ran all the way to Uncle Charlie's house and knocked once before letting herself in the back door. She had to step over a pile of newspapers on the floor and pick her way through the general chaos of the kitchen. Mama was fanatical about keeping a clean home, but Aunt Meg was 'a friend to clutter,' as Opa said.

Ginny and Marianne came running into the kitchen to greet Lizzy. Ginny squealed with excitement. "We're going to see *Dumbo!*"

"Where'd you get the money?" Lizzy asked, but she knew the answer.

"Tommy gave us both a quarter," Marianne said.

"Yeah, that's what I thought." Tom was the oldest brother in Marianne's family, and he had been hired on full-time at Caterpillar. Now that he had a job, he had a hard time denying the two younger girls anything. Sweet-talking him out of money had become their favorite pastime.

Elinor came into the kitchen. "Watch this!"

She put her hands on her hips and bit her bottom lip in concentration. She dug her right heel into the floor, then brushed back with her toe. She stomped her toe once and dropped her heel.

"Did you hear that?" She repeated the step with her left foot, this time much slower, and she stumbled. "Okay, I'm not as good with my left as I am with my right."

She tried again and Lizzy watched dutifully, but Elinor stumbled again. "Okay, I have to practice a lot more, but did you hear that?"

"What am I listening for?"

"It's called a paradiddle. It's one of the basic steps in tap dancing." Elinor repeated the step, over and over.

Lizzy reached out and took Elinor's arm. "That's great, Norrie, but we have to leave for the movie, or we'll be late." She glanced at Ginny and Marianne. "I guess they're coming with us?"

Elinor stopped her practice and snorted. "Do you believe it? We never get a break. Ma said we have to share our candy with 'em."

Lizzy shrugged. The extra nickel in her pocket made her feel generous.

The girls left the house, with Ginny and Marianne dashing ahead to pet Duke, the Snyders' Great Dane. Lizzy and Elinor kept an eye on them, but didn't try to keep them close. Talking was easier without snoopy little sisters listening in.

"Ginny told us what happened with Herta yesterday," Elinor said.

"Wait until I tell you what she did today."

Lizzy gave Elinor a detailed account of Herta's attempt to steal her money and the stray dog's brave rescue. "I hope he chased her right up her porch steps and took a bite out of her bottom before she got in the door!"

Lizzy's hopes were dashed when they arrived at the Palace Theater, and Herta was ahead of them in line with her bottom still in one piece. She glared at Lizzy, but she didn't try to talk to her or steal her money.

The four cousins filed into the darkened theater with a big tub of popcorn, a tube of M&M's, and two bottles of Coca-Cola to share. Herta and her best friend Nancy Kreiling were sitting in the front row. The curtain opened, and *Movietone News* with Lowell Thomas filled the screen.

"Don't hog the popcorn—give me some!" Ginny pulled the tub from Marianne to grab a handful. Neither of them ever paid attention to the newsreel.

"Shhhh!" Herta turned in her seat and talked over Lowell Thomas. "You're supposed to be quiet."

Ginny hit her square on the nose with a piece of popcorn.

Someone behind them clapped, and a few other kids laughed.

Herta jumped up from her seat. "I'm telling Mr. Shumacher." She flounced out of the theater.

There was more clapping, and someone yelled, "Don't come back!"

Ginny slid down in her seat. She and Marianne giggled uncontrollably. Lizzy tried to quiet them, but the girls weren't listening. Ginny knew she wouldn't get in trouble. Mr. Shumacher owned the theater, and he had a sweet spot for Ginny.

Herta was back a minute later, with Mr. Shumacher trailing behind her. He paused at the end of their aisle and gave Ginny a frown. Herta went to her seat, and Mr. Shumacher winked when her back was turned. Then he raised a crooked finger to his lips, and Ginny and Marianne settled down.

Lizzy tried to watch the newsreel. After all, someday Lowell Thomas could be describing Frank. His powerful voice told how the Nazis were taking over Europe. Somebody's "defense was demoralized." There were reports of treachery, secret agent plotting, and "Trojan horse tactics," Thomas said.

Marianne perked up at the mention of horses. "Do they use horses in the war? That's not right. Horses can't defend themselves."

Herta turned in her seat. "Don't be stupid. Don't you know what a Trojan horse is?"

Lizzy had to grab Ginny and the popcorn to keep her from pitching the rest of the tub at Herta.

The newsreel ended and another chapter of *Adventures of Captain Marvel*, "Valley of Death," kept everyone breathless as Billy Batson rescued Betty Wallace from drowning, and his alter ego, Captain Marvel, rescued the entire expedition team from a landslide.

*Dumbo* was next, and the whole theater was quiet as they watched the baby elephant with the enormous ears. The story of Dumbo and his search for self-worth flew by. Everyone teared up at the end when Dumbo was finally reunited with his mother.

Only Herta and Nancy left the theater when the credits rolled, but not before Herta threw her empty Jujubes box at Ginny. Everyone else stayed for the second showing.

The four cousins lined up in the middle of the front row with another tub of popcorn. When the second showing was over, Lizzy had memorized the words to most of the songs. She watched the reunion between parent and child for the second time with a heaviness in her chest.

*I wish all reunions could be that happy.*

# Chapter Eleven

The four girls wandered out of the theater, too full of popcorn and candy to move very fast.

Marianne moaned. "I'm not going to want any supper. I ate too many of those M&M things."

Elinor gave her little sister a stern warning. "Don't tell Ma that. She won't let us buy any treats next time."

The cousins parted ways at the sidewalk. When Lizzy and Ginny reached their corner, Lizzy turned away from home and gave Ginny a gentle push. "Go on. I'm going to walk out to the farm to get the chess set for Frank and Opa." It was kind of the truth. Opa had mentioned his chess set last night, wishing he and Frank could play a game.

The real reason Lizzy was going was to talk to Daddy. She hadn't been back, and she was sure Daddy didn't know Frank was home. She hoped that would make him change his mind about coming back with her.

Doorknob loped down the long lane from the farm house to greet Lizzy. She dropped to one knee and spent several moments petting the friendly mutt, but when his wet, slobbery tongue swiped her cheek, she stood up, pushing him away.

"Okay, that's enough. It's cold out here. Let's get to the house." She trotted up the lane with Doorknob at her heels.

Her father was standing on the porch, smiling at her. The sight of him made her heart swell, but she bit her bottom lip to keep from smiling back. If he noticed, he didn't let on. If anything, his grin got wider, and he lifted one hand in a brief wave.

Lizzy took the porch steps slowly, and she walked past him through the front door without a word.

Daddy followed her into the house. "I was wondering if I'd see you again. Sure am glad you came back, Squirt."

Lizzy's back stiffened, and Daddy made a funny noise in his throat.

"Sorry. Lizzy. Or would you prefer Elizabeth?"

Lizzy shrugged. "I don't care."

"Okay. Well, I'm glad you made it out today. I get lonely out here."

*Then come home,* Lizzy thought, but she bit back the smart reply. Instead, she said, "I was busy."

"You're getting older now. I bet you've got a lot of homework, don't you?"

Lizzy could tell he was trying hard to make conversation, but she wasn't going to help him. "Not that much."

He tried again. "Busy playing with Elinor, I bet."

"Nope."

Daddy looked away. "Well, busy or not, I'm glad you came out."

"I only came because Opa wants his chess set."

Daddy nodded. He and Opa had played chess every chance they got. Frank watched until he could play the game himself—without anyone teaching him. Lizzy suddenly remembered how surprised and proud Daddy had been the first time Frank beat him at the game.

Daddy walked to the hutch where Opa kept all his games. "Is Opa teaching you how to play?"

Lizzy took a deep breath and blurted, "Frank's home on leave, and they want to play a game tonight."

Daddy became still, his eyes closed. He finally spoke. "How long will he be here?" His voice was tight.

"A week." The words hung in the air. Lizzy clamped her mouth shut to keep from begging her father to come home with her. She refused to look at him.

Daddy pulled open the top drawer in the hutch. The chess set was on top. He rubbed one thumb over the corner of the box. He set it on the sofa, and picked up the checker board from the coffee table. He folded the board in half so all the pieces slid to the middle. He dumped them in the checkers box on the floor.

"Take this, too. You don't have a checker board, do you?"

Lizzy shook her head.

"Well, take this one then. I can't seem to win at checkers."

Lizzy frowned. "Who have you been playing?"

Daddy hesitated, but only for a moment. He laughed. "Myself. I still can't win."

Lizzy almost smiled and Daddy saw it. "Would you like to play a game?"

"No. I can't. I have to get home."

Daddy's smile wavered, and he shrugged and nodded. "Okay." He handed her the checkers box and seemed to come to a decision. "Listen, Squirt, I—I have another favor to ask you."

Lizzy waited.

Daddy took a deep breath. "I'm running out of food. If I gave you the money, would you be able to go to the Golden Rule for me? I only need a couple of things …"

He saw the look on Lizzy's face and shook his head. "Okay. It's probably a bad idea."

"Maybe I could." The words popped out before Lizzy could stop them.

"Really? What if someone asks you what you're doing?"

Lizzy shrugged. "I go to the store for Opa all the time. No one will think anything about it."

"Okay, good. I don't need much. A loaf of bread, some cheese, some beans. That should do it."

Lizzy hesitated. "I can't go tonight. I have to get home before dark. The store is closed on Sunday, so I'll have to go Monday after school."

"That'll be fine." He grinned. "I'll survive 'til then." He crossed the room to Opa's rocking chair. A worn blue coat hung on the back. He pulled a dirty coin bag from the left pocket. He took out two quarters and handed them to Lizzy.

"That should be enough." He put the coin bag back in the pocket, and the wool hat Lizzy had tucked under the bush two days earlier slipped out of a sleeve and onto the floor.

"That's your hat?"

Daddy nodded. "I thought I lost it, but I found it under a bush by the Dinky Ditch."

"I know. I found it and put it there the other day. I was going to—" She broke off, unwilling to tell her father about Gene's ragged cap.

But Daddy read her mind. "What? Does one of the boys need a hat?" He held it out to her. "Go on, take it. I don't need it."

Lizzy hesitated, and Daddy took her hand and pressed the hat into her palm. "Please."

"Gene needs a new hat real bad." She said the words so softly Daddy had to lean forward to catch them.

He smiled. "Well, good. Make sure he gets that."

Lizzy nodded. She tucked the hat under her arm and picked up the chess box. "Will you be here Monday? Where should I leave the food?"

"I'll be here." Daddy crossed his heart with a wink. "I promise. I'll be waiting for you."

Lizzy still hesitated. "Frank leaves next Friday."

Daddy understood. He nodded, but he didn't answer.

"Okay," she said. "See you Monday."

***

Lizzy arrived home as Hank banged out the front door and trotted down the front steps.

"Hey, Squirt."

When Lizzy didn't answer, he asked, "You okay? What happened?"

Lizzy opened her mouth, but no words came out.

"Come on, Lizzy, tell me. Has Herta been bothering you again?"

Lizzy still didn't answer. She was twirling the wool cap in her right hand and Hank reached out and caught it.

"Where'd you get this?"

"I found it by the Dinky Ditch when I went to Opa's house. Gene needs a new hat, so I brought it home for him."

Hank tousled her bangs. "Always the little mother, aren't you? Looking out for everyone else. Who looks out for you?"

"I don't need looking out for."

"Everybody needs looking out for sometimes." Hank messed up her bangs again and tapped the checkers box. "Tell you what. I gotta go close up at the hardware store, but I'll play you a game after supper tonight."

Lizzy finally smiled. She was pretty good at checkers. "Okay."

Hank gave the hat back and took off down the sidewalk. Lizzy went inside and slipped her shoes off on the rug.

She hung her coat and Gene's new hat on the hall tree. She carried the games to the living room. A cabinet door slammed in the kitchen.

"I don't believe it." Joe's voice carried clearly down the hall. "Pops hasn't been around for two years. Who's looking for him?"

Lizzy held her breath and tiptoed up the hall to the kitchen door.

"I don't know." Jack's voice answered. "I was at the store to get butter for Mama, and I heard a guy asking Earl if he knew where Frank Richter was." Earl was the butcher at the Golden Rule. "Earl said Frank was home from boot camp, and the guy said he wasn't looking for the son, he was looking for the father."

"What'd Earl say?" Joe again.

"Said Frank, Sr. has been gone for a couple of years. Guy said he heard he was back in town, and Earl said, 'Well, that'll be news to his family.'" Jack's voice caught in his throat. "That's an understatement."

Lizzy heard Joe slam his glass down on the table. "You don't think Pops would come back without telling us, do you?"

"Who knows?" Jack's voice was rough. "I never thought he'd leave without telling us."

A chair scraped away from the table, and Lizzy raced silently back to the living room.

The kitchen door swing open and Joe came down the hall to the living room. "What are you doing here?"

"I live here."

"Don't be smart." The words were tough, but Lizzy could hear the smile in his voice. "I meant, I thought you and the stairsteps went to see *Dumbo*. You guys always stay for two showings."

Lizzy nodded. "We did. But the movie was short, so I walked out to Opa's afterwards to get more games for tonight." She pointed at the chess and checker boxes on the sofa.

"Good idea." Joe left the room, and Lizzy gave a long sigh of relief. That was close. The twins were brutal when they caught her spying on them.

She climbed the stairs to her bedroom, and her thoughts went back to the conversation she had heard.

*Who else could be looking for Daddy? Officer Mueller looking for him is bad enough. Who else is out there?*

## *Chapter Twelve*

An hour later, Lizzy made her way to the kitchen to help Mama get supper. She pushed through the swinging door. Mama sat at the table, holding a cup of coffee, and the counter tops were free of pots and pans and bowls.

Mama saw her confusion and smiled. "Change of plans. Aunt Meg is having family supper tonight. Everyone wants to see Frank."

Lizzy gave a happy sigh. Family supper would be a welcome break after the last few days. The family laughed as much as they ate, and they usually ate a lot when they went to Aunt Meg's house. Uncle Charlie and her two oldest cousins, Tom and John, all had jobs that allowed them to buy the extras Mama couldn't afford. Aunt Meg always had dessert, and sometimes Tom and John bought a Coca-Cola for everyone.

"What are we taking?"

"Bread and apples. Go get your coat on." Mama drank the last of her coffee and set the cup in the sink. "Frank and Hank will meet us there when Hank gets off work."

Ginny waited at the door, bouncing up and down on her toes. Gene stood quietly by his sister, staring out the window. He pulled his ragged wool hat out of his coat pocket and had to pull hard to get the sides to cover his ears.

Lizzy smiled, eager to give Gene the new cap. "Wait till you see—" she began.

Gene gave a quick shake of his head. The look in his eyes stopped her.

Mama didn't see the brief exchange. She came up behind them, buttoning the wool coat she wore every winter. "The temperature's dropping. I think winter might get here early this year."

***

Seventeen people crowded around the long table that started in the dining room and ended in the living room. There were two tall soup kettles of chicken and noodles on the table. Another kettle held an enormous mound of mashed potatoes.

Joe nudged his cousin Bill and pointed at the food. "Who are we eating tonight?"

Marianne crossed her arms in a pout and her eyes teared up. She always cried when one of her chickens was butchered.

Aunt Meg answered. "I think that's Harriet."

"Harriet?" Marianne uncrossed her arms. "Well, that's okay. Harriet was kinda mean. She was always pecking at the other chickens."

Opa shook his head. "Never a good idea to name your food."

Uncle Charlie nodded in agreement. "That's what I tell her. She won't listen."

A bottle of Coca-Cola sat in front of every place setting, and with the loaves of bread and the basket of apples Mama brought, there was plenty to eat. The smell of Frank's favorite pie, custard with nutmeg, floated out of the kitchen.

"How long do you think Roosevelt is going to sit on his can and do nothing?" Uncle Charlie addressed Frank as Mama and Aunt Meg filled bowls, first with potatoes, then chicken and noodles.

Frank glanced at his mother, but he answered honestly. "Not too much longer, I hope."

Mama and Aunt Meg exchanged glances, and Frank changed the subject.

"How's work at Caterpillar?"

Tom answered the question. "Word is we're gearin' up to make tank parts instead of tractors."

Aunt Meg glared at her son and set his bowl down with a bang.

Uncle Charlie winked at Frank. "How 'bout those Cubs?"

Frank hid a smile and took a bowl. "Wait 'til next year."

The chicken and noodles were gone in short order. Several of the boys had a second or a third slice of bread, and all of them crunched through at least two apples. When the meal was over, Opa stood up from his chair.

"Gene, Bill, take the girls into the parlor and play games or listen to the radio," he said.

There was a sudden silence at the table. Gene glanced at Mama, and she nodded. Bill started to protest, but Uncle Charlie stopped him.

"You heard Opa."

Lizzy began to clear her place. Aunt Meg placed a gentle hand on her arm.

"We'll clean up, sweetie," she said with a smile that didn't look anything like her. "Go on."

They left the table and headed for the door, but Ginny stopped. "Is this about dessert? Isn't there enough pie for all of us?"

Her comment brought shouts of laughter from the boys.

Uncle Charlie reached out and gave her a hug. "Of course there's enough, Squeaker. But we've got grown-up stuff to talk about. We'll all have pie when we're done jaw-jackin' in here. That sound okay?"

Ginny nodded, but she cupped her hands around her mouth and whispered loudly in his ear. "Joe and Jack aren't really grown-ups, you know."

That brought a roar of laughter from everyone, and Ginny darted past the twins before one of them could grab her and tickle her.

★★★

Ginny was still complaining while Gene set up the Monopoly board. "What do they want to talk about that we can't hear?"

"You heard Uncle Charlie. Grown-up stuff. Probably stuff about the war."

"What about it?" Ginny was persistent.

"How should I know?" Gene tried to distract her by choosing the shoe for his playing piece.

She forced his hand open and took the shoe. "Is Frank going to be in the war? Is that what they're talking about?"

Gene sighed. "I don't know. If there is a war, Frank will probably be in it. But that's a big if."

Lizzy knew the truth. War was coming. The only question was when.

Elinor gave Lizzy a sympathetic look, but Lizzy looked her right in the eye and raised her eyebrows. *There's more going on than talk of war,* her eyes said.

Elinor took the hint. "I don't want to play *Monopoly.* Lizzy and I are going upstairs."

Bill frowned. "Well, then take these two with you, and Gene and I will play *Camelot.*"

Marianne grabbed the tiny *Monopoly* car and placed it firmly on the board. "Pa said to play games with us."

Elinor spoke over her shoulder on her way out of the room. "We took them to the movies today. You can play *Monopoly* with them tonight. Come on, Lizzy."

"At least turn on the radio before you go."

Elinor flipped the knob of the Philco, and the theme song for *The Shadow* filled the room. She and Lizzy were up the stairs in a flash.

"What's wrong?" Elinor shut her bedroom door.

Lizzy didn't answer right away. She went to the register on the far side of the room and knelt beside it. She put a finger to her lips. "You were right. Daddy's in trouble. There's a stranger in town looking for him."

Lizzy opened the register slowly, cringing when the metal creaked. She stretched out on the floor and put her ear to the grate. She listened to see if voices from the dining room carried.

Elinor knelt beside her. The voices coming through sounded far away and nasally, like the Munchkins' voices in the *Wizard of Oz*. Elinor whispered in Lizzy's ear. "You can hear better in Tom and John's room. Come on."

"What if they catch us?"

"We'll have to be real quiet. The stairs squeak, so we'll know if anyone's coming."

Elinor opened her door without a sound, and the two girls tiptoed down the hall to Tom and John's bedroom. Elinor tossed a pair of pants and several socks covering the register onto the nearest bed. Both girls knelt on the floor, and Elinor opened the register with great care. Suddenly Lizzy could hear Opa clearly.

"So what's this talk about some out-of-towner lookin' for Frank?"

Lizzy strained to hear Jack's mumbled answer. "Some guy was at the Golden Rule asking for Pops. Earl told him he'd been gone for quite a while."

Uncle Charlie spoke. "Did you see the man? Did you recognize him?"

"No, he had his back to me, and he left pretty sudden after that. I tried to follow him out of the store, but by the time I got outside, he was driving off in a big ol' Packard."

"Could be a war buddy lookin' for your dad," said Opa.

"I don't think so. I don't think he knew Pops. He pronounced our name wrong. He said Rich-ter. Earl said 'you mean Ric-ter?' and the guy said, 'probably' and spelled it for him."

"Did he look like a policeman?" Frank asked the question. There was a shocked silence.

Jack answered. "No. I mean, he didn't have a uniform on or anything."

"Really, Frank." Aunt Meg could hardly get the words out.

"Well, why else would someone come here looking for him if he's not in trouble? If he had to sneak out of Chicago, this is the first place they'd look."

Hank spoke, and the anger in his voice gave Lizzy goosebumps. "So what if he's here? I don't care if he's in trouble or not. He better not show up at our house. I'll lock him out."

Mama spoke for the first time. "That's not your decision to make, Hank."

There was a heavy silence. Mama spoke again. "How about some pie, Meg?"

## Chapter Thirteen

Sunday morning, Lizzy squirmed between Frank and Hank in the fourth row of St. Paul's Lutheran Church. There was a time when the whole family fit easily in one pew, but those days were long gone. Ginny used to sit on one of the boys' lap, but now she was too big for that, so she was smashed between Joe and Jack.

The pew creaked and shifted. Lizzy glanced down the row. Joe and Jack were restless, and she watched Joe reach over Ginny to stick a wet finger in Jack's ear. Jack responded with a kick that missed Joe and hit Ginny. She squeaked in surprise.

Lizzy turned around to see if Elinor and the rest of the family were in their regular pew. Elinor gave her a grin and a finger wave. Lizzy knew Herta and her family sat on the other side of the church, but she didn't bother to look for them.

Before she turned to face the altar again, Lizzy saw a man she didn't recognize in the second-to-the-last pew. His long sleeves and open collar stood out in the sea of black-suited men with thin black ties. Lizzy turned quickly and stared straight ahead. *Is that the stranger looking for Daddy?*

Pastor Bortel began the Old Testament reading. "The text for our sermon today comes from the book of Esther."

Lizzy always enjoyed Pastor Bortel's sermons. He had a melodious voice, and he wasn't afraid to get loud when he needed to. The story of Esther was one of her favorites. She knew Esther was beautiful, but Lizzy was more impressed by her love for her people. When Haman got hung on the gallows meant for Mordecai, Lizzy always felt a twinge of satisfaction. She wanted to concentrate on the sermon, but she couldn't focus, knowing the stranger was in the back of the church.

She looked over her shoulder once, praying Mama or Opa wouldn't notice. The man in the back was listening to the pastor's words, but when he saw Lizzy looking at him, he raised his eyebrows and gave her a wink.

Lizzy jerked back around. Hank leaned over and whispered in her ear, so low his lips barely moved. "What is going on with you?"

"Nothing."

Twenty minutes later, Queen Esther ratted Haman out and Pastor Bortel bellowed, "'Who is he, and where is he who would dare presume in his heart to do such a thing?'"

As the sermon drew to a close, Lizzy risked one more look at the man in back. *Who is he, and how dare he presume in his heart to spy on my family?* Whoever he was, he was listening intently to the sermon.

They seldom got through church without one minor upheaval, and today Ginny dropped the offering plate. Coins rolled under the pew in front of them, and Ginny, Lizzy, and Gene scrunched down to pick up the nickels and dimes rolling on the wooden floor.

One last hymn and a silent prayer later and church was over. Lizzy pushed past her siblings to get out of the pew. She searched for the stranger, but he was gone. She practically ran to the back door, not caring if Mama or Opa saw her. When she got outside, he was nowhere in sight.

"What are you doing?"

Lizzy jumped. Hank and Frank were behind her.

Hank studied her face. "You were antsy through the whole service, and you're never antsy. What's going on?"

Lizzy gave in. "Okay, look. Elinor and I listened to you guys last night when you were talking about the stranger who was looking for Daddy. I think he was in church this morning."

Frank nodded. "I saw him too."

"He winked at me during the service."

"Well, where'd he go?" Hank asked.

Lizzy shrugged. "I tried to get out here as fast as I could, but he's gone." She paused. "Should we go look for him?"

Frank smiled, and Lizzy was struck by how handsome he looked in his Marine dress blues. How much he looked like Daddy. "And if we find him? What do we say? 'How dare you come to church?'"

Lizzy sighed. "You're right."

Frank put his arm around her and gave her a hug. "If he's looking for Pops, he'll come to the house. If not, he's none of our business."

Lizzy knew they had to find this man, but she couldn't tell Frank or Hank why. She gritted her teeth. How long did her promise to Daddy last?

Hank's voice was stern. "Okay, one last time. What is going on?"

Lizzy frowned. "Nothing's going on. But aren't you curious? Don't you want to know why this guy is here?"

"No. Not if he has anything to do with Pops." Hank turned and walked away.

Lizzy looked across the field behind the church. She could see Opa's house in the distance, a tiny blur. Lizzy thought if she squinted hard she could probably see Daddy staring out the window.

Opa stumped up behind them. He followed Lizzy's gaze across the field. "Sure wish I could get out to my place."

"What do you need now, Opa?"

"I need my place." Opa took a breath. "But until then, I need more of my books. Your mama has some good ones, but there's nothin' like Zane Grey. And I need a pair of good socks. Had to wear my work socks to church today." He lifted his pant leg and showed them a yellowed sock. Opa's one good suit was old and shiny where the cloth was worn, but the sock was worse.

"I'm sure the Schimmelpfennings would drive you out there," Frank said.

"No, they do enough what with haulin' me back and forth to church. I'll send one of you kids out there this afternoon."

Lizzy volunteered. "I'm happy to go for you, Opa."

Frank shook his head. "Not by yourself. Not with this stranger hanging around town. I'll go with you."

Lizzy knew she was in for an argument, so she thought fast. "Aren't you supposed to visit Mr. Musch this afternoon?"

Her brother frowned. "Then Hank can go with you."

"Hank's taking Jane to the movies." She glanced around the church yard. Gene was talking with Otto while the whole Schimmelpfenning family waited patiently for Opa.

"Gene can go with me."

Frank shook his head. "No. The twins."

"The twins will whine the whole time and they'll be grumpy if they don't get their nap."

Frank laughed. "Yeah, sometimes I think they're six, not sixteen."

"And Gene is as big as the twins now. You said so yourself."

Opa interrupted the exchange. "Well, you two make a decision. I gotta get goin'. Oscar's waitin' for me." He turned and walked down the sidewalk to the car.

Gene opened the passenger door for his grandfather and helped him into the front seat next to Oscar Schimmelpfenning, Sr. His son, Oscar, Jr., was driving. Oscar Junior's wife and their two boys, Oscar the Third and Otto, squeezed into the back seat. The shiny DeSoto pulled out of the drive.

Gene joined his siblings. "What are you guys talking about?"

"Will you walk out to Opa's house with me this afternoon?" Lizzy asked.

"Sure."

Frank frowned at the too-quick and eager answer. "Okay, now I sound like Hank. What's going on?"

"Nothing."

Their simultaneous denial made Frank shake his head. "Right." He turned to Gene. "You know about the strange guy in town, don't you?"

Gene nodded. "He was in church today."

"Keep an eye out for him. Now let's go eat lunch."

★★★

An hour later, Gene followed Lizzy out the front door. She turned at the bottom of the steps and watched him pull on his ragged hat.

"Why don't you want to wear the hat I brought home for you?"

He was silent for a moment. "Where did you find it?"

"On the bank of the Dinky Ditch. Under a thorn bush."

Gene watched her closely, and she met his gaze. She knew if she blinked or looked away, he'd know there was more to the story. When she didn't budge, he shook his head.

"So why won't you wear it?" she asked again.

"You know why."

"No, I don't. Tell me."

Gene faced her, his expression sad. "Pops had the same one."

Lizzy blinked hard, and she couldn't help but think, *He still does.*

Gene saw her reaction. He reached out and grabbed her arm. "Lizzy, I know you know something. You've been acting too weird lately. If you know where Pops is, you have to tell me. Is he back in town?"

Lizzy didn't answer, but an unexpected tear rolled down one cheek. Gene shook her arm. "Lizzy, tell me! If that guy is in town to find him or arrest him, Pops probably needs help, and you can't help him all by yourself. Tell me. Is he at Opa's house?"

Lizzy nodded.

Gene let go of her arm and headed for the street. "Come on. We have to hurry. That guy has a car, and he could see us and follow us. We have to get out of town and out of sight before that happens."

Instead of walking through town and taking the road to Opa's house, Gene ran down Paw-Paw Street. He was taking the shortcut Mama had forbidden them to use.

"Gene! We can't go this way. We'll get grounded."

"I'm not gonna tell—are you?"

Lizzy groaned under her breath. She followed Gene down Paw-Paw, past Ernie's house, past the Vogels' house, all the way back to St. Paul's. They cut through the empty church parking lot and into the corn field behind. She could see Opa's house again in the distance.

The stubble caught at Lizzy's feet, and she stumbled several times. Gene kept glancing over his shoulder.

"Hurry up, Lizard. No one's going to see us, but that doesn't mean we can stroll."

They made it through the field and up Opa's lane without being seen. Gene charged up the porch steps and tried the door. Locked. He pounded hard on the wood frame, and the glass in the window rattled. No one pulled the curtain back. Lizzy found the key in the post and unlocked the door.

Gene burst into the parlor, shouting at the top of his lungs. "Pops, where are you? Pops, it's me, Gene! It's okay! Where are you?"

There was no answer. The two children searched the whole house, including the cellar. No Pops.

Gene dropped to the sofa in the living room and covered his eyes with one hand. Lizzy knew he would be embarrassed if he cried, so she spoke fast.

"His stuff is still here. His book and his cup are on the nightstand in the bedroom. He'll be back. We can wait if you want to."

Gene shook his head. "If we're still gone when Frank gets home, he'll start to worry and come looking for us." He looked up. "I'm not sure what would happen if he came out here and found Pops."

Lizzy agreed. "So we'll keep this to ourselves. At least for now." When Gene didn't answer, Lizzy persisted. "It's our secret, okay?"

"Okay."

Lizzy walked down the hall to the bedroom to get a pair of Opa's good socks and two more Zane Grey books. When she came back, Gene was still on the sofa. She stuffed the socks in her coat pocket, and handed Gene the books.

He stared at them, his shoulders slumped. "I suppose we should go."

Lizzy's eyes burned at the sadness in his voice. "I have to come back out tomorrow," she told him. "I promised

Daddy I'd go to the store for him after school. You could come with me. I'm sure he'll be here."

"I have basketball practice. Coach says anyone who misses a practice has to have a good reason or they don't play in the next game. What reason would I give him?"

"I don't know." She paused. "I'll tell Daddy you were here."

"Will it matter?

He stood up and walked out the front door. Lizzy followed her brother outside. She pulled the door shut, locked it, and put the key back in the post. Gene was already halfway down the lane. Lizzy ran to catch up with him. Neither one said a word all the way home.

## Chapter Fourteen

On Monday after school, Lizzy stood in the last aisle of the Golden Rule. She had a fresh cut chunk of cheddar cheese and a loaf of Wonder Bread in one hand. Now she debated over the canned beans on the shelf. Which did Daddy like best—Campbell's or Heinz?

"Campbell's is cheaper," said a voice behind her. Lizzie turned. Ernie Fisher was holding a broom and wearing a too-large butcher's apron looped over his neck. The apron's skirt was pulled above his knees, with the ties wrapped around his waist and knotted in front. "Your mama bought Campbell's last week."

Lizzy reached for the can of Heinz beans. "When did you start working here?"

"Last week. Engle Ben knows Ivan and Vernon will be joining up soon, so he decided to start my training while they're still here to help me." Ivan and Vernon were Ernie's older brothers.

When Lizzie didn't respond, Ernie nodded at the cheese in her hand. "Your mama told me your grandfather and the twins won't eat cheese."

"The rest of us love it." Everyone else *did* love it, but Mama only bought things that everyone would eat. She hoped Ernie was too new to know that.

"I thought your mama baked all your bread." Ernie was staring at the loaf of Wonder Bread.

Lizzy bit back a sharp reply. She put the Heinz beans back and pulled a can of Campbell's off the shelf before she answered. "She doesn't have much time to bake with Frank home." That was a lie, but Lizzy didn't know what else to say. Then she stopped.

*Don't be a dope. He's just trying to talk to you!*

She turned back to Ernie and gave him a shy smile. "With Frank home, lots of things are different."

Ernie smiled back. "He looked great in his dress blues at church yesterday."

Lizzy nodded. "Mama cried when she saw him."

Ernie shrugged one shoulder. "Yeah, well, you know moms."

A shout from Engle Ben made both of them jump. "You done sweeping, boy?"

"Almost." He turned to Lizzy. "Gotta go. See you tomorrow." He gave an awkward wave and pushed the broom down the aisle.

Lizzy hurried to the front of the store. The grocery bill was 45 cents, so Helen, Engle Ben's wife, gave Lizzy a nickel back from her two quarters.

Lizzy pushed out the front door of the Golden Rule and it slammed shut behind her. The wind was brisk, so she set the small bag of groceries on the sidewalk and buttoned her coat. Otto Schimmelpfenning leaned against the side of the building, munching on an apple.

"Hey, Otto."

Otto nodded, his mouth too full of apple to answer.

Lizzy reached for her groceries when the familiar sound of rubber on concrete whooshed behind her. She snatched the paper sack off the ground as Herta zoomed by her and grabbed for it. She got one corner, and the sack tore. The beans, cheese and bread all tumbled to the ground.

Herta braked at the corner and turned to ride back up the sidewalk. Lizzy stuffed the groceries in her school bag. Herta stopped her bike so close Lizzy had to step off the sidewalk to avoid getting her toes run over.

"What have you got?" Herta pulled at the school bag, but Lizzy's grip was firm, and she jerked the bag out of Herta's grasp.

"None of your business. Why do you care about my groceries?"

"Maybe you've got something in there I like." Herta pulled at the bag again.

Lizzy held on to the bag with one hand and grabbed the handlebars on Herta's bike with the other. She pushed her backwards off the sidewalk.

Herta stumbled off the bike and crashed to the ground, taking the bike down with her. She struggled to pull her foot out from under one pedal and untangle herself. She finally got to her feet.

"You're going to pay if you broke my bike." Her face was red, and her mouth was pinched.

Lizzy scowled. "I didn't hurt your bike. I've seen you fall off a dozen times. There are probably a million things already wrong with it."

Otto swallowed another big bite of apple. "Yeah, Herta." He snickered. "You're kind of clumsy."

Herta gave Otto a withering glance. He wasn't impressed.

The door to the Golden Rule opened. "What's going on?" Engle Ben stepped out and pulled a Marlboro from the pack in his front pocket.

Herta faked a loud, snotty sniff. "Elizabeth shoved me off my bike. I caught my foot under the pedal, and now it hurts real bad." Her voice trailed off in a pathetic whimper.

"I see." Engle Ben lit his cigarette and took a deep pull. He studied both girls. "Let me get this straight." He blew smoke out of the side of his mouth. "Did Lizzy do that before or after you ripped open her grocery sack and pulled on her book bag?"

Herta's theatrics vanished. She glared at Engle Ben.

He wasn't impressed either. "Get on home, Herta. And don't ride on the sidewalk, you hear?"

Herta was already pushing her bike down the walk. She jumped on the seat and turned to stick her tongue out at Engle Ben before she rode away, staying on the sidewalk until she was out of sight.

"Ornery little snot." Engle Ben turned to Lizzy. "You okay?"

Lizzy nodded.

"She'll come back, you know."

Lizzy shrugged. "I'm used to it. She doesn't scare me."

Otto made an impressive shot with his apple core into the Golden Rule's burn barrel. "I'll walk with her to the corner," he told Engle Ben.

Lizzy sighed. She wasn't going home, at least not yet, but she couldn't tell Otto that. They left the store and headed up Andrew Street.

"Gene told me your dad might be back in town," Otto said. "That true?"

*So much for keeping a secret*, Lizzy thought. "Why would Gene say that?"

"No reason, I guess." Otto stopped at the corner of Andrew and Paw-Paw. He glanced down Paw-Paw and shook his head. "Man, she's persistent, isn't she?"

Herta was riding her bike in slow circles in the next block.

"Come on. I'll walk you the rest of the way."

Lizzy shook her head. "I'm not afraid of her. Go on home."

"You sure?"

Before Lizzy could answer, the Black Hawk Grove police car pulled onto Paw-Paw and stopped next to Herta. Lizzy and Oscar could see the window roll down, and Officer Mueller leaned out to say something to Herta. He reached out his window and grabbed her arm. She pulled free and took off on her bike. She rode past Otto and Lizzy with a spiteful look, but she kept riding until she turned the corner two blocks away and disappeared.

Otto turned toward his own street. "Looks like you got lucky this time." He waved at Lizzy before he cut through the Vogels' yard.

Officer Mueller passed her, and she gave a brief nod as he drove by. He was staring at her, and she was suddenly frightened he would follow her instead of Herta. Then she mentally pinched herself.

*Why would he follow you? You're being a dope.*

She walked slowly down her street. When she heard the police car turn the corner, she doubled back and took the forbidden shortcut out to the farm.

★★★

She reached Opa's house without seeing anyone. She ran down the lane, expecting Doorknob to come loping around the corner. But there was no sign of the goofy dog anywhere.

She ran up the porch steps, turned the knob, and almost hit her nose on the door. Locked. She took the spare key from the porch post and opened the door. Daddy must be gone again. Where was he? He told her he would be here.

She tucked the key in her coat pocket and walked through the parlor, through the living room, and down the hall to the kitchen. She dropped her book bag on the kitchen table next to a coffee cup half-full and still steaming. Suddenly she heard a voice singing the familiar words to "You Are My Sunshine."

*Does Daddy have a radio? And what is it with that song?*

No. It wasn't a radio. The singing came closer, and it was accompanied by a thump, step, thump, step. She wheeled around. A man with one leg and two crutches stood in the kitchen doorway. They stared at one another for several moments before the man spoke.

"Who are you? What are you doing here?"

Lizzy grabbed her book bag from the table and ran for the back door.

"Hey!" Lizzy could hear the man thumping behind her. She flew out the door and down the steps.

"Wait! Are you Lizzy?" He pushed the screen door open and thumped onto the porch.

Lizzy stumbled to a halt and turned around. "Who are you?"

"I'm ..." The man looked confused. "Don't you know me?"

Lizzy stared at him. "No."

"My name's Myron."

"Myron? Myron Minser?"

The man nodded.

"But ..." A cold chill ran down Lizzy's spine and she stared at him. The man she had seen in the picture with Daddy stared back. "I thought you were dead."

Myron grinned. "Not hardly."

"Where's my dad?"

"Who?"

What was wrong with this man? "My dad." Her voice quivered. "Your best friend."

Myron only stared at her, his eyes blank.

"My dad!" She backed away, her voice raising to a frightened yell. "I want my dad!"

Myron Minser's blank stare gave way to anger, and he thumped down the porch stairs after her. "Git outta here, you hear me? Leave me alone!"

The back door flew open, and Daddy was there, next to Myron, his hand on the man's shoulder, his voice quiet. "Myron, it's okay. This is Lizzy."

Lizzy watched Myron's anger slip away like a whiff of smoke. "Where you been, Frank?"

"I was in the cellar," Daddy said. "Come on, let's go back inside and see what Lizzy brought us to eat." He turned Myron around and tried to help him up the steps. Myron shrugged out of Daddy's grasp and used his crutches to pull himself up one step at a time until he reached the top.

Myron opened the screen door and spoke over his shoulder. "Your daughter Lizzy's here."

"I know."

"Pretty little thing. Looks like her mama."

# Chapter Fifteen

Lizzy watched the two men make their way through the kitchen. She climbed the porch steps and stopped outside the screen door.

Daddy led Myron to the living room. Thump, step, thump, step. Then a softer, heavier thump and the groan of the sofa springs as they bent under Myron's weight.

"You stay here, buddy, and I'll go see what I can get you to eat. You're hungry, aren't you?"

"Hungry enough to eat a horse."

"Will a cheese sandwich do?"

"Guess it'll have to."

Daddy came back to the kitchen and motioned Lizzy inside. She stepped through the screen door and watched the hall.

"It's okay, Squirt." Daddy lowered his voice. "Don't be scared of Myron. He won't hurt you."

"What's he doing here? I—I thought he died in the war."

"That's what we all thought." Daddy slipped Lizzy's school bag off her shoulder and set it on the table. He pulled out the bread and cheese and beans. He opened the bread and took out several slices.

"Daddy." Lizzy's voice shook. She reached out and took the bread slices from her father. "What is going on?"

Daddy leaned on the table with both hands. He took his time answering. "It turns out ... Myron has been alive all these years. The military had him listed as missing in action and *presumed* dead." Daddy stopped and swallowed hard. "They were wrong." His voice broke.

Lizzy set the bread on the table and waited.

After a moment and a deep breath, Daddy continued. "From what we can piece together of the things Myron remembers, he was a prisoner of war. They held him in Laon, France, for a time, then transferred him to Camp Rastatt, near Baden, Germany."

He pulled out a chair and sat down, hard. "He has no memory of the war ending or coming home. Somehow, he ended up in Chicago."

Lizzy blinked back unexpected tears at the stab of pity she felt for the strange man in the next room. "How—how could the military just *lose* him?"

Daddy shook his head. "I don't know. But you can imagine how I felt when I saw his picture in the newspaper the day your grandma died. He was in line at a soup kitchen on State Street. His leg was gone, his hair was long and ragged, but it was Myron."

He stood up and searched the drawer behind him, pulling out a cheese slicer. "I was shocked. I couldn't think straight." He cut a slice of cheddar off the block of cheese. "I don't know if you can understand this, Squirt, and I don't expect any of you to forgive me. But I had to find him. He saved my life in the war." He slammed the cheese slicer down on the table. "He saved my life."

Lizzy watched his gaze slip back to something dark, something she knew he couldn't talk about.

She reached out and touched his hand. "You could have told Mama. Or Opa. They would have understood."

Daddy nodded. "They would have. But the problem was me."

Lizzy watched him put the cheese between two slices of dry bread. He took a knife and cut the sandwich in half.

"I couldn't get a job." He shook his head. "No, that's not true. With my temper, I couldn't keep a job. My boys were doing more to provide for our family than I was." His voice dropped. "I was humiliated."

"But Daddy, a lot of people lost their jobs. We understood."

Daddy gave her a sad smile. "I know, Squirt. At least, I know *now*. Back then, I couldn't see it. I thought all of you would be better off without me."

Lizzy couldn't speak. Finally she whispered, "How could you believe that?"

He sighed. "When I thought Myron died in the war, I blamed myself. When the Depression hit, and I lost not one, not two, but *three* jobs, I blamed myself. Then I saw Myron's picture in the paper, and I felt like I was getting a second chance. I could go to Chicago, find Myron, get a job, prove I wasn't ... worthless."

Lizzy squeezed her eyes shut. "You're not worthless, Daddy."

"I know, sweetheart. I had to wander around for a couple of years to figure that out, but I finally did."

She opened her eyes and took a breath.

Daddy continued. "I told you before that I stayed at Pacific Garden Mission. They were patient with me. They helped me. They finally made me see my problems weren't up here." He pointed to his head. "They were in here." He pointed at his heart.

"They have a saying at the mission, 'Let go and let God.' So I did. I finally realized nothing I did made any sense if God wasn't behind it."

Lizzy nodded. "Pastor Bortel talks about that almost every week."

Daddy smiled, and it warmed his eyes, just the way Lizzy remembered. "I guess you've been listening more than I ever did. I could have saved myself a lot of trouble if I'd known that when I was eleven.

"I kept looking for Myron," he continued. "Took me a while, but I found him. Now he's in trouble." He stopped to correct himself again. "We're *both* in trouble, and I can't abandon him, or let them put him away like a crazy man."

Lizzy lowered her voice. "He *is* a crazy man. He was chasing me. He was yelling at me."

"Did you yell first?"

Lizzy bit her bottom lip and nodded. "He wouldn't tell me where you were. He was scaring me. What's wrong with him?"

Daddy rubbed his forehead with one hand. "Myron's not right. He doesn't remember much, and when he does, he usually remembers wrong. He can't handle yelling or anger or loud noises. He's had a tough time since the war."

"But that was years and years ago."

"Sometimes these problems never go away. At least, not without help. He needs help dealing with them."

"Doesn't he have family? Let them help him."

Daddy shook his head. "His father died when he was young, and his mother died when we were in high school. I haven't been able to find his sister. I know he had an uncle, and Myron says he lives right across the border in Indiana. That's why I brought him here. I'm trying to find someone who knows his uncle in Indiana."

"Why do you have to hide?" Lizzy was still confused. "There are probably lots of people who knew Myron growing up. They could help you look."

Daddy started a second sandwich. "It's not that simple, Squirt. There's more to the story."

"So tell me the story." Lizzy crossed her arms and stared at her father.

He smiled. "Guess I have to. You're not going to let me off the hook, are you?"

Lizzy shook her head.

"Okay," he said. "When I found Myron, he was a patient in an asylum in Chicago. It was an awful place. I asked them to release him into my care, but they refused. So I had to ... improvise."

"What does that mean—improvise?"

"It means some things happened I'm not proud of."

Daddy tapped the table with the cheese slicer, and hesitated. Lizzy wondered if he was going to continue. Finally, he did.

"I had a pretty heated discussion with two of the guards about his living conditions. Myron heard us—he misunderstood the argument, and he attacked them to protect me. I got him under control, but they were hurt. Not bad, but bad enough." He shook his head at the memory.

"I convinced them to tell their supervisor I was the one who hurt them. Myron had never been violent before, and I didn't want that going in his medical file, or things would get worse for him."

Daddy sighed. "But the doctors didn't believe the guards. They sent Myron straight to solitary, and they were going to try a new therapy on him—something called shock therapy. A volunteer who's been a good friend to Myron knew where I was staying. He came and told me what was going to happen.

"I couldn't let them do that to Myron. Their security is pretty lax, so the next day, this volunteer left a few doors open. I was able to sneak Myron out. I hoped the hospital had better things to worry about than one missing mental patient."

Lizzy's heart started to pound.

Daddy saw her expression. He gave a worried glance down the hall. "What?"

"Daddy, someone is looking for you."

"Who?"

"Joe heard this guy asking about you in the Golden Rule. I don't think the guy knows you. He pronounced our last name wrong. Joe said he had a picture he showed to Officer Mueller."

Daddy stared at the cheese slicer and turned it over in his hand. Then he straightened up and finished making another sandwich.

Lizzy watched him, waiting for him to speak.

"Have you told anyone I'm here?"

Lizzy hesitated. "Elinor. And Gene."

"Aw, Lizzy ..."

"Daddy, Elinor won't tell anyone."

"But Gene..."

"Daddy, Gene wants to help you! We came out yesterday to see you, but you weren't here. He was so disappointed. I know he'll do whatever he can for you."

"What about the older boys?"

Lizzy couldn't look her father in the eye. "I don't think we should tell them."

"That's what I thought."

He paused, and Lizzy knew what was coming next.

"No—don't leave—please don't leave!"

Daddy didn't answer, and Lizzy hurried on. "I don't care what you did. If you were trying to help Myron, the people who are looking for him will understand, won't they?"

"No, Squirt, they won't." He put a tender arm around her shoulders, and she grabbed him and hugged him hard. He pulled her onto his lap, and she buried her face in his shoulder. She tried to stop the tears soaking his shirt, but he smelled the same as she remembered, and she cried harder.

When she finally stopped, Daddy pulled a handkerchief out of his pocket. She blew her nose.

"The three of us are the only ones ..."

Daddy stopped her. "Officer Mueller suspects. He drives down the lane once or twice a day. He came up on the porch yesterday. I barely got the front door locked and Myron out of the living room before he was looking in the window."

"But you can hide in the cellar ..."

Daddy stopped her again. "It won't work, Squirt. Not long term. I have to get Myron out of here, someplace safe. Most people don't understand what war can do to a man. He's not right in the head, but he can't help it. And I'm not going to let him waste away in an asylum. He deserves better."

There was a loud creak, then thump, step, thump, step. Myron appeared in the kitchen door. "Hey, Frank, where's that cheese sandwich?" He gave Lizzy a warm smile. "Who's the little girl?"

"This is my daughter, Lizzy."

"Pretty little thing. Looks like her mama."

# *Chapter Sixteen*

Daddy made Myron three cheese sandwiches before the man was finally full. Myron ate slowly and chewed carefully, and he always swallowed before he spoke. He asked Lizzy all kinds of questions while he ate. *How old are you? Who's your teacher? You like school? Who's your best friend? You like to read? You got a boyfriend?* Lizzy answered all his questions. She finally relaxed when Myron teased her about her 'no boyfriend' answer.

"Can't hardly believe that." He winked at Daddy. "You're a looker, like your mama. 'Course, your oma was a beauty, too. How's she doing these days?"

Lizzy looked at her father.

Daddy spoke. "Mama died a few years back, Myron."

Myron finished his sandwich. He seemed to think about Daddy's answer. Then he said in a matter-of-fact tone, "No, she didn't."

Daddy didn't argue. He put the bread in the breadbox, and he wrapped up the cheese and opened the ice box. There was no ice, but he stuck the cheese inside anyway.

"I just saw her at DeSutter's hardware store," Myron continued. "I needed a new tire for my bicycle, but I didn't have the money, so she bought one for me. You remind me to pay her back next payday."

Daddy smiled. "You were twelve when she bought you that tire."

Myron ignored him. "Bike rides real good now. But I need to pay her back." He turned to Lizzy. "Charlotte, we got to pay back Mrs. Richter, so I'll give you the money when you go for your piano lessons."

Lizzy gave her father a panicked glance. She knew her grandmother used to give piano lessons, but who was Charlotte?

Daddy's voice was gentle. "Your sister stopped taking piano lessons thirty years ago."

Myron frowned. "Well, she never liked to practice much anyway. But that don't mean we won't pay Mrs. Richter what we owe her."

Daddy closed his eyes. "Mama won't take your money," he said.

Myron stood up from the table and stretched, balancing perfectly on his one good leg. Then he grabbed his crutches from against the cabinet. "Maybe I can work around the house for her. Hate to be in debt to anybody— you know that, Frank."

Daddy nodded. "She'd like that."

Myron smiled. "Maybe I'll clear out that flower bed in back for her, plant roses or something." He looked down at his crutches, and confusion made the smile waver. "Well, I'll do something." He turned and left the room.

Lizzy watched him thump down the hall. Her father was watching her, and he reached out to squeeze her shoulder. "You understand now?"

Lizzy nodded. "What are you going to do?"

"I don't know. But it's not your worry, Squirt. You better get on home."

Lizzy picked up her school bag. "Will you be here tomorrow?"

Daddy looked her square in the eyes. "Yes. I promise I won't leave without telling you."

Lizzy walked down the hall and into the living room. Myron lay stretched out on the sofa, his good leg hung over the end. His eyes were closed, but his voice stopped her.

"Don't you forget to practice now, Charlotte. We're gonna go see Aunt Hulda and Uncle Albert, and they'll want to hear you play."

"Okay." She shut the front door behind her.

Lizzy took her time walking home. There was too much to think about. With Myron Minser back, everything changed. In her mind's eye, she could see the picture of Daddy and Myron Mama kept in the hutch. Both were young, about the age Frank was now. The fact was, Daddy looked exactly like Frank Jr. in that picture.

And Myron. In the picture, Myron was taller than Daddy, heftier, with an ornery gleam in his eye. The grin on his face always made Lizzy grin back. She thought Myron and Daddy looked like they had a secret they weren't telling anyone. The thought sobered her. Now they did. Except she was in on it, and she'd dragged Elinor and Gene in with her.

Should she tell Frank? What about Hank? Hank didn't care if he ever saw Daddy again. Easy-going Hank wouldn't even talk about Daddy coming back. What would he do if he knew Lizzy had known about Daddy all along—that she had been helping him?

There were too many questions, and they made Lizzy's head hurt.

*What do I do, Lord? I don't think there's much more I can do to help. Daddy needs more than a can of beans and a loaf of bread.*

Lizzy turned down Paw-Paw Street and realized she didn't remember the walk home.

Now there were other things to worry about. A black Packard sat in the street in front of the Embrees' house. The Embrees lived three houses down from the Richters, and they didn't have a car. Was this the car Joe had seen drive away from the grocery store? Was this the stranger looking for Daddy?

Lizzy slowed down and crossed the street to stay as far from the car as possible. The driver rolled down the window and called out to her.

"Are you one of the Richter children?"

She glanced at the man. She recognized him from church. She tried to ignore him, but he called again.

"Excuse me? Are you a Richter?"

"I don't think that's any of your business."

The man got out of the car. He shut the door and rested against it, his arms crossed. "You are a Richter. I saw you at church yesterday. Can I ask you a couple of questions?"

Lizzy was almost even with the car now. She walked faster. "I don't think so."

The man held up both hands as if he was surrendering. "I'll stay right here. I only want to talk."

Lizzy finally stopped. "I have a question of my own," she blurted. "What are you doing here? Why are you looking for my father?"

The man lowered his hands and smiled. The smile seemed genuine, and his face looked friendlier. "How do you know about that?"

Lizzy didn't answer.

The man sighed. "Okay. Doesn't matter. But I *am* looking for Frank Richter, Sr. Is he home?"

"He left two years ago."

"I didn't ask when he left. I asked if he was back."

"Why should I tell you?"

"I have some questions for him. He's not in trouble."

Lizzy frowned. "I don't believe you. Go away." She started walking.

"Wait—stop. Please."

Lizzy stopped.

"Okay. Let's start over. My name is Cap Campbell."

Lizzy frowned. "Is that your real name?"

The man grinned. "I was a captain in the Army in the Great War. My men called me Cap. It stuck."

Lizzy shrugged and nodded. "Okay."

Cap continued. "I had the opportunity to meet Frank in Chicago, but he's not there anymore. I need to find him. There are things we have to talk about, but I'm not here to get him in trouble. Honest."

"I don't believe you."

Cap shook his head. "Well, that's too bad. So you won't tell me? Is he home?"

Lizzy gave one determined shake of her head. "No. He's not home."

Cap smiled. "Now I'm the one who doesn't believe you."

"I don't care. He's not home."

"Hey!"

Lizzy jumped at the sound of Frank's voice. She turned to see Frank and Hank barrel full speed up Paw-Paw Street. Frank's expression was intense and his face was red. Hank had a baseball bat in one hand.

Cap Campbell sighed, but he didn't move. "Great. Just great."

# Chapter Seventeen

Frank crossed the street running, but he slowed to a stop when he got close to the Packard. Hank stopped right behind him.

Frank put up a hand with his thumb out and gestured toward their house. "Lizzy, go home."

Lizzy backed up, out of Frank's sight, but she stayed where she was.

The older man pushed himself away from the car. He walked toward Frank, his hand extended. "I'm Cap Campbell. You must be Frank Junior. You look just like your father."

Frank grabbed the hand and held on. "I don't care who you are." His voice was like ice. "I want to know why you're watching my family."

Cap pulled his hand free and flexed his fingers with a slight smile. "I'm looking for your father. We have a common friend, Myron Minser."

Frank's eyes narrowed. "Were you in the war with my dad and Myron?"

"No. I only met Myron a few years ago, but we've become good friends."

Hank's grip on the bat tightened. "That's a lie. Myron Minser is dead."

Cap's eyebrows raised, and he shook his head. "No, he's not."

Frank gave the man a wary look. "What are you talking about?"

Cap studied the two boys' faces. "Well, that explains a lot. You don't know."

"Know what?" Hank banged the front fender of the car with the bat for emphasis.

"Hey!" Cap walked to the front of the car and examined the fender for damage. Satisfied there was none, he turned back to the boys.

"Myron was missing in action at the end of the war. He was a POW, and when he was released, he was ... a different man. Damaged. He got shipped back to the States, but he didn't know his own name for a long time, or who his family was.

"Myron was admitted to an asylum in New York," Cap went on, "and he stayed there for a few years. Bits and pieces of his memory started to come back, and he remembered his name and that he was from Illinois, so he got relocated to Chicago. Different people looked for his family off and on, but unfortunately, most asylums are overcrowded and understaffed. Sometimes, patients aren't treated well. Myron was no exception. He ran off several times."

Cap walked back and opened the driver's door. He reached across the front seat and came out with a well-worn book. He opened the book and pulled out a news clipping.

"This picture was taken one of the times Myron escaped. Your father saw the picture in the newspaper and recognized him right away."

Cap handed the news clipping to Frank. Frank studied the photo, and Hank peered over his shoulder. "I'm pretty sure this is what prompted him to come looking for Myron."

Frank's voice was quiet. "He saw this the day Oma died. We were out at Opa's house, and Pops was reading the paper. I asked for the sports page, but he told me to wait my turn. I thought he was upset about Oma, so ... I waited my turn. I found the paper after the funeral, and there was a page torn out."

Hank took the clipping. "The day we buried Oma, Pops had a fight with Opa. I couldn't hear what it was about, but there was a lot of yelling. Pops was gone the next morning."

Frank nodded. "I heard it, too. Opa would never tell me what it was about, but I got the feeling he thought Pops's leaving was his fault."

Lizzy's chest felt heavy. Everyone had heard the yelling. Did Opa really blame himself?

Lizzy held out her hand, and Hank gave her the clipping. A hand-lettered sign that read "Soup Kitchen" hung over a long line of men, women, and children dressed in shabby clothes. A one-legged man, far back in the line, was turned to face the camera. He balanced on two crutches. He had a big grin on his face, and Lizzy could see the resemblance to the photo Mama had in the hutch. It was Myron. She handed the clipping back to Cap.

"Your dad spent a long time looking for Myron. He wouldn't give up." Cap tucked the clipping back in the book and gave the book to Lizzy. "This belongs to him. He loaned it to Myron. If you happen to see your dad, maybe you could give it back to him."

Lizzy took the book without a word. *Lone Star Ranger,* another Zane Grey novel.

"What makes you think Pops and Myron are here?" Frank asked.

Cap smiled. "I never saw Myron as happy as he was the day your dad showed up at the asylum. All he could talk about was the good times he had with your dad and Annie. I gather they were all pretty close?"

Frank shrugged. "I guess. We only heard stories about him. Opa once said Oma considered him another son."

Cap nodded. "Myron felt the same way. He can't remember his own parents, but he sure remembers Rudy and Clara."

"You still haven't answered the question," Hank said. "Why do you think they're here?"

Cap shrugged. "Where else would they go?"

"If Pops was back, why wouldn't he come home?" Frank asked. "None of us have seen him."

"Maybe he's protecting you."

"From what?" Hank asked.

Cap took a deep breath. "The police are looking for your dad and Myron."

"Figures." Hank slammed the bat down on the road.

Frank reached out and grabbed it. "Stop it. That's the only bat the twins have. You're going to crack it." He turned to Cap. "Why are the police looking for them?"

"They've been charged with assault."

"What?"

"It's not as bad as it sounds," Cap said. "Your dad had reasons for what he did. Myron can't pass a competency test, so he's a ward of the state. Frank didn't like the way Myron was being treated, so he asked to have Myron released into his custody. The state refused, since Frank's not a family member.

"When Frank confronted some of the staff about Myron's treatment, the discussion got heated and ended in a fight with two of the guards. Things got worse instead of better for Myron, and your dad came back the next day and snuck him out of the asylum."

Hank frowned. "Are the guards okay?"

Cap nodded. "They're fine. One's got a broken nose and the other has some pretty sore ribs. They weren't going to press charges, but the asylum has a legal obligation to report an incident like that to the police. So now your dad and Myron are wanted for assault, and Myron is considered unstable and possibly dangerous."

"What's your connection to all of this?" Suspicion was clear on Hank's face. "Are you with the police? The asylum?"

Cap shook his head. "I'm not with the police, and I only volunteered at the asylum. Like I said, I consider Myron a good friend. I want what's best for him. And I've never seen him happier than when he was with your dad."

He opened his car door and put one foot on the running board. "I might have unlocked a few doors the day your dad came to get Myron. I'm here because I want to make sure I didn't make a mistake. I'd like to find them before I have to head back to Chicago, but in case I don't, you know the whole story now, so maybe you can find a way to help them."

When no one answered him, he leaned on the open door and spoke one last time. "War can do awful things to a man. Sometimes that man never recovers. Sometimes he does. Helping Myron was your dad's way to recover. He's a good man."

The three siblings watched Cap Campbell drive away. The boys were silent, and Lizzy hoped they would stay that way.

No such luck. Frank stared at Lizzy for several moments. "Is Pops at Opa's house?"

Lizzy didn't answer.

"Is he?"

Lizzy swallowed hard and stayed quiet.

Frank muttered a bad word. His hands were two fists, so tight the hair on his knuckles stood up. "How long has he been back? Why didn't you tell somebody? How could you do this, Lizzy?"

His anger made her chest hurt. "Don't make me take sides, Frank."

"Aw, Squirt." He took a deep breath. "I'd never do that."

Lizzy held her ground. "I won't help you get Daddy arrested."

"All I want to do right now is talk to him," Frank said. "Figure out what we're going to do."

They started the short walk home. Hank was staring straight ahead, refusing to look at her.

Lizzy took Hank's arm to stop him. "I just wanted to help Daddy. You said everyone needs someone to look after them sometimes."

Hank didn't answer. He shook off her arm and walked faster. Lizzy didn't try to keep up.

## Chapter Eighteen

Gene came running down the porch steps as soon as they got close to the house. "Hey, Frank, you'll never guess who's here to see ..." He stopped short at the sight of the three somber faces. He risked a quick look at Lizzy.

Frank saw it. "So you know too?"

Gene opened and shut his mouth. "Know what?"

Frank swore again, softly. "What's wrong with you two?"

Neither Gene nor Lizzy answered.

Frank gave up. "Okay, who's here to see me?"

"The whole Budke family."

Hank's expression lightened. "Ben and Bart are here?" The Budke family had lived next door to the Richters for many years, and the two oldest boys in each family had become close friends. The Budkes moved to Peoria when Mr. Budke took a big-wig job with Caterpillar two years earlier.

"Yep. Everyone's waiting for you in the dining room."

Frank looked at his three siblings and pointed a long finger at each one of them. "Not a word to Mama. Got it? We still have a lot to figure out, but it's going to have to wait until tomorrow. Tonight, we have a good time, okay?"

The younger siblings all nodded, and Hank straightened his shoulders. "Shouldn't be too hard. Ben and Bart are always a good time," he said.

Hank was right. The reunion with the Budkes was loud and full of laughter. The adults listened and laughed along as the boys reminisced. They ate cold fried chicken, compliments of Mrs. Budke.

When the Budkes asked Frank about his service in the Marines, Mama shooed the younger siblings out of the room. "You've heard all this already, and I know you have homework to do. Tell the Budkes goodbye, and get to your rooms."

Lizzy was the only one who left without complaining. She got her book bag from the hall table and climbed the stairs. She waited for Gene on the landing.

He took the stairs two-at-a-time when he saw Lizzy waiting for him. "What happened? Did Frank and Hank see Pops?"

Lizzy shook her head. "No. They only found out about him because of Cap Campbell."

"Who?"

"He's the guy who's been looking for Daddy. You saw him in church."

"You met him?"

Lizzy nodded. "Come on, I'll tell you everything before Ginny gets up here. Can we talk in your room?"

"Sure." Gene led her down the hall, closed his door and leaned against it. "Just to make sure no one sneaks up on us."

Lizzy told him everything, beginning with her scary encounter with Myron Minser.

Gene's mouth dropped. "He's alive?"

Lizzy nodded. "He's the reason Daddy left."

It took some time for Lizzy to get through the story, mainly because Gene interrupted with question after question.

"Where has Myron been? ... What took so long for Pops to find him? ... How bad is his memory? ... So Mueller knows Pops is back because this Cap guy is looking for him?"

And his last, scary question. "Is Pops going to jail?"

Lizzy could hardly swallow around the lump in her throat when she thought of Daddy in jail. "I don't know. If Mueller finds them at Opa's house, he could arrest him, I guess. Daddy said Myron's got family right across the state line. I think he wants to find them and leave Myron with them."

"But what will happen to Pops?"

Lizzy didn't answer. No matter what happened to Myron, Daddy would still be in trouble.

"Maybe Frank can figure a way out of this." Gene didn't sound hopeful.

Lizzy rubbed her eyes. "I don't know if Frank wants to help Daddy. And I think Hank would just as soon see him in jail."

A sudden bump on the door and a loud "Hey, what's going on? Let me in!" startled them both. Gene turned and opened the door.

Ginny pushed past her brother and flopped on his bed. "What are you guys doing in Gene's room?"

"Lizzy wanted help with her math. You got spelling to do?"

Ginny drooped at the mention of spelling. "Yeah." Then she brightened. "Will you help me?"

"Sure. Go get your book, and I'll quiz you."

Lizzy followed Ginny to their bedroom. Ginny dug through her new book bag for her speller, then raced back down the hall.

Lizzy scooted back on her bed and rested against the headboard. She pulled out *Great American History* and tried to concentrate, but she fell asleep before the end of the first paragraph.

***

The next morning at breakfast, Lizzy and Ginny were alone at the table. Gene and the twins always left early for school.

Mama was humming as she pulled another bowl out of the cabinet. The kitchen door swung open, and Frank came in and pulled out a chair. Mama filled the bowl with oatmeal, set it in front of him, and started talking.

"Engle Ben offered us the use of his car today. He thought we might want to drive to Havana to get some watermelons. The crop was late this year, and ..." She stopped when she saw Frank's surprised expression. "Oh, honey, I'm sorry. Did you have something else planned for today? I was so excited when Engle Ben offered, I accepted without thinking about asking you first."

Frank smiled at her. "No, Mama, that's fine. It's just been a while since I've driven a car. Wouldn't want to wreck Engle Ben's pride and joy."

Mama laughed. "Oh, shush. You're a wonderful driver. He suggested we keep going and get that new variety of apples at Curtis Orchard in Springtown. I do get tired of Jonathans all the time. And there's a new diner on the west side of Springtown. Since I'm going to have my Marine all to myself, I thought I would treat him to a nice lunch ..."

***

Lizzy sat through class that day without hearing a word Mrs. Himmel said. Fractions and Jefferson's Great Bargain were too much to think about when she knew Daddy could be arrested at any moment. When the last bell rang, Lizzy grabbed her book bag and coat and ran for the door. She didn't want to talk to anyone.

No such luck.

Elinor stood waiting for her outside. "Where are you going? I think Herta's been talking because there are a lot of kids who know her dad is looking for your dad. What are you ..." She stopped. "What is it? What aren't you telling me?"

Lizzy pulled her cousin down the school steps. She gave her a quick rundown of all that had happened since Sunday. Elinor's response was the same as everyone else's.

"Myron Minser is *alive*?"

Lizzy nodded. "He needs help, and Daddy wants to get him to Indiana, but if Mueller gets into the house before Daddy can get him out of town they'll both be in big trouble." She paused. "I'm going out to the farm right now to let Daddy know what's going on. Frank and Mama are probably on their way home from Springtown, so I have to get out there before Frank does. I need to warn Daddy."

"Warn him? Why? Don't you think Frank will help him?"

Lizzy shrugged. "I don't know. Frank and Hank weren't happy to hear Daddy was back, much less why he left in the first place. I know Hank would gladly turn him in."

Elinor shook her head. "No, Lizzy, you're wrong. Hank might act like he's mad, but I think that's his way of protecting himself." Elinor paused. "I heard Pa tell Opa he found Hank in the tool shed bawling his eyes out the day after Uncle Frank left."

Lizzy swallowed hard. "Hank?"

Elinor nodded.

Lizzy had a sudden memory of Hank and Daddy out in the yard, building Mama a new hutch. Lizzy could still hear them laughing as they worked. "They always laughed at the same dumb jokes."

Elinor nodded. "Hank will come around. I know he will."

"I hope he comes around before Mueller puts Daddy in jail." She pressed her book bag into Elinor's hands. "Would you take this home with you? I'll come get it when I get back."

"Sure."

"Thanks. I shouldn't be long."

## Chapter Nineteen

Lizzy took her usual route to Opa's house. Once she was out of town, she left the road and climbed down the embankment to the Dinky Ditch. She followed the little creek all the way to Hobbs Hill. She was ready to climb back up to the road when the sound of a car made her freeze.

She dropped to the ground and lay flat, hoping whoever was in the car couldn't see her. The low rumble of the engine grew louder, and she stayed flat until she heard the car pass. She waited until the sound faded, then scrambled up the embankment to the road's edge.

The car was going fast, shrinking in the distance, leaving a cloud of dust. Lizzy was positive it was Officer Mueller, going out to check Opa's house again for signs of Daddy and Myron.

Her heart was pounding, and she had a hard time taking a deep breath. Would Daddy be able to get out of sight with Myron before Officer Mueller saw them?

Lizzy stood on the side of the road, unsure of what to do. She heard the sound of another car coming up behind her. She whipped around, knowing she couldn't get out of sight before whoever was in this car would see her.

She held her breath until Engle Ben's Ford rumbled up next to her. Frank was driving, and Hank sat next to him.

Frank rolled his window down. "Lizzy! What are you doing out here?"

"I wanted to talk to Daddy before you saw him." Lizzy swallowed hard. "He knows you're not happy he's back. I wanted to warn him you're probably going to—to turn him in."

Frank scowled. "I told you. I'm going to talk to Pops before I do anything." He tilted his head toward the back seat. "Get in."

Lizzy opened the car door and scooted inside. "Officer Mueller is already on his way out there." She barely had the door shut before Frank took off down the road.

They pulled up to the house. Officer Mueller stood on the front porch, peering through the parlor window, his hands cupped around his eyes to block out the sunlight. He didn't hear them until Frank, Jr. skidded to a stop on the dirt lane.

Mueller straightened and turned around, a grim expression on his face. His frown deepened when Hank jumped out of the car. Hank slammed the door and charged up the porch steps two at a time.

"Hank!" Frank got out of the car, and his sharp voice stopped his brother inches short of the police officer.

Mueller nodded at the boy. "Good afternoon, Hank." With his thick accent, the name came out "Haaank," and Lizzy saw "Haaank" bristle.

"Deee-ter," he answered, imitating the older man.

Officer Mueller had two thick blond eyebrows that met up and wiggled like a furry caterpillar when he frowned. Hank's response made the caterpillar do a dangerous dance.

Mueller took a step towards the younger man and their faces were nose to nose. Without breaking eye contact with Hank, Mueller spoke. "Hello, Fraank. Welcome home."

"Thank you, sir," said Frank. "How can we help you?"

Frank's polite tone and use of the word sir seemed to pacify the officer, because he stepped back from his face-off with Hank. Then he gave the boy an up and down glance that even Lizzy could see was an insult. Hank's fists clenched.

"There has been a report there are vagrants in your grandfather's house," said Mueller.

"Who gave you that report, sir?"

Mueller ignored the question and asked one of his own. "May we look inside and check to see if this is true?" Before Frank could answer, the officer turned the knob on the front door. It was locked.

Mueller looked at the boys. "Do either of you have a key?"

"No." Frank answered for both of them.

Lizzy suddenly remembered tucking the key in her coat pocket the day before. She had to clench her fists to keep from checking to see if the key was still there.

Fortunately, Mueller didn't question her. "Where does your grandfather keep a spare key?" He reached a long arm above the door and ran his hand across the header. No key.

Hank was still in fighting mode. "We don't need you to check the house. We can do it ourselves."

Mueller shrugged. "I am sure you can, but vagrants can be dangerous. I am trained to deal with them. I would not be doing my job if I did not help you." He picked up the crock by the door and checked underneath. No key. He scanned the length of the porch and his eyes fixed on the notch in the beam. He walked over and put two large fingers in the empty space. No key.

Hank spoke again. "If a trained police officer can't find a key to get in the house, what makes you think a vagrant could?" He was still glaring at the older man.

Mueller gave him a tight smile. "Vagrants seldom go in through the front door. Let us walk the perimeter and see if there is any damage. A broken window, perhaps? Or another entry that has been forced open. If there are vagrants, there will be something."

Frank nodded. "Sure. That's a good idea. Let's go."

Lizzy sucked in her breath. What was Frank thinking? What if Daddy hadn't locked the back door?

Frank ignored Lizzy's panicked look and Hank's loud and exasperated sigh. He led the way around the house, checking every window ahead of Mueller. All of them were closed, with no sign of any damage. They came to the porch steps in back and Mueller went ahead of Frank to try the door. Locked. Mueller checked above the door and under the braided rug bunched up against the door frame. No key.

They finished their walk around the house, checking all the windows on the west, but none of them were open or broken. They came full circle and stopped at the bottom of the front steps.

Frank faced the officer. "I don't believe you need to worry, sir. There's no sign of damage. But we'll go home and tell Opa about these supposed reports you've received."

Mueller's eyes narrowed at the word "supposed," and he gave Frank a hard stare.

Frank only smiled. "If Opa is worried, we'll come back with the key. Thanks for your concern."

Mueller ignored Frank's obvious dismissal. "I have another question." He stopped and looked at each of them in turn, focusing last on Lizzy. Her heart was pounding out a jungle beat, but she returned his stare without blinking.

"Elizabeth, Herta tells me you have made several trips to this house in the last week. Why? Did you have a key then? If you did, why are your here now, without a key? I find that unusual."

Lizzy opened her mouth to respond. Her mouth was dry and she had no idea what to say. Then a black blur raced around the corner of the house.

Lizzy broke into a relieved laugh. "There he is! Doorknob, where have you been? Opa has been worried about you."

Frank and Hank both whipped around to see a scrawny black dog running full tilt at Lizzy. Hank's mouth dropped open, but Frank caught on right away.

"Hey, Doorknob!" At the sound of Frank's voice, Doorknob slid to a confused stop, then gave a joyous bark and leaped at Frank, knocking him back. His paws were on Frank's chest and he was trying to lick his face.

"Good boy." Frank tried to calm the excited dog, but Doorknob barked and licked and barked some more, until Frank had to force him to the ground. "Sit," he commanded, and Doorknob sat. All of him but his tail. That was thumping furiously.

Lizzy looked at Officer Mueller. "Doorknob's a stray Opa kept around. I've been coming out to check on him. I haven't seen him the last few days, so I told Frank and Hank, and they got Engle Ben's car so we could bring him home with us if he was—you know—hurt or something." The lie finally wound down. Lizzy was too embarrassed to look at her brothers.

Officer Mueller stared at her for several seconds. He held his hand out to the dog. Doorknob sniffed the outstretched fingers cautiously. His tail stopped thumping.

Mueller withdrew his hand. "I am glad he is all right." He walked to his car, climbed in, and turned around in Opa's front yard. He drove away without a backwards glance.

Doorknob's tail started thumping again, and Frank scratched the dog's head. The dog nuzzled into Frank's hand and gave him another lick.

"Nice to meet you, too, Doorknob." Frank knelt in the dry grass and rubbed his thumbs over the dog's ears. Doorknob whined with pleasure.

There was a tapping noise on the porch window. All three siblings looked up to see their father's shadow half-hidden behind the plain white curtain. The shadow disappeared and the front door opened.

Doorknob left Frank and trotted up the porch steps. Daddy stepped aside to let the dog in. Doorknob stopped and sniffed his hand. Then he looked back at Frank, confused.

Lizzy raised a hand in greeting, and Daddy gave her a sober wink, but his attention was on the two young men he hadn't seen for more than two years.

"Hello, boys."

Hank turned without a word and walked back to the car. He climbed in and slammed the door.

Daddy sighed. "Frank, we need to talk."

Frank nodded. "You got that right."

"Son—" Daddy began, but Frank interrupted him.

"Not now. Mueller will be watching for us. If we don't leave now, he'll be back."

"Okay." Daddy nodded. "But soon."

"Yeah. I'll come back later."

Daddy took a deep breath. "As soon as you can. Please."

Frank didn't answer. He walked back to the car and held the front door for Lizzy. She sat between her two silent brothers and waved goodbye to Daddy as they drove away.

# *Chapter Twenty*

The ride home was too long and too quiet. Frank stopped in front of their house. "I'm taking the car back to Engle Ben. I'll be right back."

Hank got out and slammed the door behind him. He took the porch steps two at a time.

Lizzy stayed in the car. "Could you take me down to Uncle Charlie's house? I left my book bag with Elinor after school."

"So Elinor knows about Pops, too." It wasn't a question. Frank rubbed the steering wheel with his thumb. "How could you tell Elinor and not tell—"

Lizzy interrupted him. "I'm sorry. I wanted to tell you, but Daddy made me promise I wouldn't tell anyone in our family." Frank's lips pursed into a thin line, and he stared out the window. "But I had to tell someone, so I told Elinor. Are you mad at me?"

Frank's eyes closed. "No, Squirt, I'm not mad."

Lizzy's hopes rose. "Are you going to help Daddy?"

"I didn't say that."

"But—"

"Lizzy, things were different for me when Pops left. You're too young to understand."

"No, I'm not. I know you had to do all the things Daddy wasn't here to do, like keep the twins out of trouble and help us with homework and take Mama to Doc Elisa when she got real sick ..." Her voice broke, but she kept going. "You had to be everything for everybody. You were the one who held us all together. I won't ever forget that."

Frank stared at her. "I guess maybe you're not too young."

Lizzy swallowed hard, willing him to understand. "But it's *Daddy*."

Frank sighed. "Yeah, Squirt, I know."

He put the car in gear, and they made the short trip north to Uncle Charlie's. Lizzy slid across the seat and out the door, but Frank stopped her before she shut it.

"Squirt?"

"Yes?"

"When you get home, don't say anything to Mama. I haven't told her anything yet."

Lizzy nodded. "I won't say a word, trust me."

Frank smiled. "Oh, I trust you, all right. You're good at keeping quiet."

"I'm sorry, Frank."

He gave her Daddy's wink. "I know. It's okay." He pulled away and Lizzy watched until he turned the corner onto Maple Street.

Lizzy went around the house and through the back door. Elinor sat at the kitchen table, reading.

Norrie put a finger to her lips, and her voice was soft. "Tom and Dave are in the living room I heard them talking about Uncle Frank when I got home. Everyone knows something is going on, but no one knows what."

Lizzy sat at the table and whispered in her cousin's ear. "Frank and Hank saw me on the way to the farm. They saw Daddy. Hank wouldn't talk to him. And now Hank won't talk to me."

She squeezed her eyes shut to keep from crying. "I only wanted to help, and now I think I've only made things worse. For Daddy. For all of us."

Elinor pulled Lizzy's book bag out from under the table. "Well, take this and go home. So far, no one knows I know what's going on, but if they find out, I'll be in hot water, too."

Lizzy took the bag, her expression glum. "Frank knows."

Elinor groaned and put her head on the table.

Lizzy patted her arm. "I'll ask him not to tell anyone. And I won't tell you anything else. I'll keep you out of it from now on."

Elinor looked up, scared. "What else is there to tell?"

"You don't want to know, remember?"

Lizzy slipped out the back door and walked up John Q. as fast as she could, praying none of her other cousins saw her.

When she got home, she left her shoes on the rug and hung her coat on the hall tree. She went upstairs and took longer than usual to change into her everyday clothes. Then she dropped to her bed and sat for several minutes, staring at nothing. With a sigh, she finally stood up and went downstairs.

Hank sat at the table with an uneaten peanut butter sandwich in front of him. He stood and shoved his chair back when he saw her.

"Hank ..."

"What?" Without waiting for an answer, he said, "I can't believe you did this to us, Lizzy."

Lizzy snapped. "How was I supposed to know what to do? When should I have told someone? The day Frank came back, so I could ruin his homecoming? Who should I have told? Uncle Charlie, so he could have Daddy arrested? You tell me, what should I have done?"

"Seems to me you've already done it! You told Frank you didn't want to take sides, but you already have." Hank slammed his hand on the table. "Pops is going to leave again. You know he is. How about you go with him?"

Lizzy turned and ran from the room. She flew up the stairs, slammed her door, and threw herself on the bed, face down.

There were loud footsteps on the stairs and then the door burst open. "Lizzy!" Hank pulled her up from the bed and wrapped her in a hug. "Lizzy, I'm sorry."

Lizzy pounded on his chest and tried to push away, but Hank held on, and she finally gave up. "What about those verses on forgiveness and love you quoted at me?" Her voice was muffled by Hank's shirt. "Daddy's changed. He really has. Doesn't he deserve forgiveness and love?"

"I'm sorry, Squirt." He swallowed. "I can't—I don't ..." His voice died out and he let Lizzy go.

She pushed herself back to the headboard. "You don't understand."

"What's to understand? He left us. Now he's back. Are we supposed to pretend nothing happened? I can't do that."

"You don't understand," Lizzy repeated.

They both heard the front door open, and Lizzy scrambled off the bed and ran to the top of the stairs. Frank looked up and Lizzy gestured to him. "Come here. There's more I need to tell you."

Frank took off his shoes and coat and trudged up the stairs. Lizzy waited until he reached the top, then went back into her room and leaned against her desk.

Frank stood inside her door, his expression unreadable. "What?"

She took a deep breath. "Myron is at the house, too. And he needs help."

Frank shrugged. "I figured he was there. And yes, I know he needs help, but—"

"You don't understand."

Hank gave a disgusted grunt. "You keep saying that. What don't we understand?"

"Cap told you he's changed, but he didn't tell you how much. There's something wrong with him."

"What do you mean, wrong?" Frank asked.

"I don't know how to explain it. He acts strange. Not all the time. Sometimes he's fine, and other times he forgets everything. Where he is, who he is, what year it is, everything. And sometimes he gets angry. Daddy says he came back from the war like that."

"You mean like shell shock?" Hank asked.

Lizzy frowned. "I don't know what that means. But Myron beat up the guards, not Daddy."

"Look, Squirt," Frank said, "it doesn't matter who did what. Pops and Myron shouldn't be hiding. If they don't turn themselves in, if they don't step up and tell the authorities exactly what happened, nobody will believe them when they're finally caught. And they will get caught."

He took a deep breath. "I'm not sure how I feel about Pops right now, but if you're right, I don't want him to go to jail for something he didn't do. And I feel sorry for Myron, but maybe an asylum is the best place for him."

Frank left the room. Hank followed him.

Lizzy flopped back down on her bed and lay still for a long time. Frank's words bounced around in her thoughts until her head hurt.

"*... I don't want him to go to jail for something he didn't do ... sorry for Myron ... an asylum is the best place for him ...*"

Lizzy knew what she had to do. She went to the top of the stairs and listened. She could hear Frank and Hank talking in the living room. She couldn't make out all the words, but she heard enough to know they were making plans to talk to Officer Mueller. She only had a few minutes before they would realize she was gone. She had to get back out to Opa's as fast as she could.

# Chapter Twenty-One

Lizzy ran down the porch steps. Herta was on her bike in the street, watching the house.

"Why are you here?" Lizzy didn't expect an answer, and she didn't wait for one. She stepped past Herta and headed down Paw-Paw Street.

Herta glided past her and turned back slowly, brushing Lizzy in the process. Lizzy sidestepped her and kept walking. Herta rode around her, behind her, and glided past again. This time, when she turned in front of Lizzy, Lizzy grabbed the handlebars and pushed hard. Herta was expecting it. The bike dipped, but she kept her balance. She recovered and made another complete circle. She pulled directly in Lizzy's path, forcing her to stop.

"My dad's going to arrest your dad, you know." The words were a statement of fact, not a challenge or a taunt. "It's his *job.*"

Lizzy nodded. "I know. We'll see what happens."

The coat Herta wore was halfway down her arm, and her bruise had turned an ugly greenish-yellow. She saw Lizzy looking at it, and she pulled the sleeve up with a jerk. "*My* father would never desert our family." Her voice cracked.

Lizzy stared at her. Was she going to cry? Maybe Hank was right. Lizzy didn't know what was going on in Herta's house. Maybe Herta had reasons for acting the way she did. Maybe she really didn't know any better.

All Lizzy knew was she was tired of this battle. What good had it done?

She shrugged and said, "You're right. I guess there are lots of ways fathers can hurt their kids."

She turned and hurried down Paw-Paw Street. She could hear Herta riding slowly behind her. When she reached the church, she faced the other girl. Herta skidded to a stop beside her.

"I really wish you wouldn't follow me."

"I can if I want."

The two girls stared at one another. For the first time Lizzy could remember, there was no smirk on Herta's face, no meanness in her eyes.

Lizzy broke the silence, her voice soft. "Please. I have to help my father."

Herta's hand strayed to the bruise under her coat sleeve. Her eyes grew moist. She blinked hard and gave Lizzy a short nod.

Lizzy turned and took the shortcut through the corn stubble to Opa's house. When she was to the crossroads, she looked behind her. Herta was a small figure, staring after her.

Lizzy raised her hand in a brief wave. Herta waved back.

Lizzy ran to Opa's house. She bounded up the porch steps and tried the door. Daddy peered out from behind the curtains. He unlocked the door and pulled her into the house. They both started talking.

"Frank's going to talk to Officer Mueller—"

"I can't find Myron—"

They both stopped.

"Myron's gone?"

Daddy nodded. His forehead was creased with worry. "What did Frank say?"

"He thinks you and Myron should turn yourselves in. He said maybe Myron would be better off at the asylum."

Daddy frowned. "You told Frank Myron was here?"

Lizzy shrugged. "He kind of knew already, after we talked with Cap Campbell."

"Cap's here?"

"That's who's been looking for you."

The worry lines faded. "Did Cap have a car?"

Lizzy nodded. Then she brightened. "Maybe he came out and got Myron."

"Maybe." Daddy's look was thoughtful. "Cap was one of the few people at the asylum who treated Myron right." Then he shook his head. "But why would they leave without telling me? That makes no sense."

"And why would he think to look out here?" Lizzy thought for a moment. "Maybe Officer Mueller told him this was Opa's house, and he put two and two together. I bet that's what happened." She searched Daddy's face. "Do you think that's what happened?"

"I don't know, Squirt. I can't believe they'd take off without telling me their plans."

"How long has Myron been gone?"

"I don't know for sure. Before you kids came by, I went down to the Dinky Ditch to check my pole lines. I was hoping to have fish for supper. I was gone an hour, maybe longer. Myron was lying down in the south bedroom when I left. When I came back, he was gone. Then the three of you showed up with Mueller, so I hid in the basement."

"Cap *had* to come pick him up," Lizzy said. "How could Myron get away with only one leg?"

Daddy moved to look out the window and took a deep breath. "Here comes Mueller now."

"What are you going to do?"

"I guess I'll have to talk to him."

"But ..." Lizzy swallowed hard. "What if he arrests you?"

"If he does, I want you to go home and tell Mama everything."

"Everything?" Lizzy's voice trembled.

Daddy smiled. "I know your mama can be fierce sometimes, but don't you think it would be better if she heard the truth from you instead of Officer Mueller?"

"I guess so."

Officer Mueller pulled to a stop in the yard and shut off the engine. He walked up the steps and came straight to the window, peering inside.

Daddy opened the front door. "Hello, Mueller." He opened the door wide and gestured to the officer to come in the house.

Mueller took his hat off and stepped inside. When he saw Lizzy his eyebrows squished back into a caterpillar, but he said nothing.

He turned to Daddy and came right to the point. "Why have you been hiding from me?"

"Just trying to protect my friend."

"You are wanted for assault, and Mr. Minser must be returned to the asylum in Chicago."

"Good luck with that. Myron's gone."

The officer glared at Lizzy and her father. "Do not lie to me."

"I'm not lying. You can search the house. I honestly don't know where he is."

Mueller's gaze was suspicious. "Stay here."

Lizzy dropped to the sofa. Daddy stared out the window. They listened as Officer Mueller opened and shut doors all through the house. Daddy began to hum, so softly Lizzy could hardly make out the tune. When she did, her breath caught in her throat.

"Why do you like that song so much?"

The humming stopped abruptly. "What?"

"That song. "You Are My Sunshine." Why do you like it so much?"

Daddy stared at her, curiosity in his eyes and a half-smile on his lips. "You remember that?"

Lizzy shook her head. "But Mama does."

"Ahh." Daddy's gaze went back to the window. "I like the song because it made me think of your Mama the very first time I heard it—two years ago. I told her I had seen a lot of gray skies since I came home from the war, but she was the sunshine that made me happy."

"That's ... sweet."

Daddy smiled. "Yeah, well, she didn't think so. You know your mama. She has a Bible verse for everything. She told me my focus was in the wrong place, and then she quoted Psalm 27:1 at me."

Lizzy nodded. "'The Lord is my light and my salvation— whom shall I fear'?"

The cellar door banged open, and Officer Mueller's heavy footsteps clumped down the wooden staircase.

Daddy went on. "She told me the Lord was the light that should make me happy. It only made me mad when she said it. That was right before I left home. But now I know she's right. It's become one of my favorite verses." He winked. "But I still love the song."

Officer Mueller returned to the living room. "You will come with me to the village hall for questioning."

"Am I under arrest?"

Officer Mueller glanced at Lizzy. "Yes."

Lizzy stood up and realized her knees were shaking. Daddy put his arm around her shoulders.

"Can we give Lizzy a ride home first?"

Mueller nodded.

"Will you look for Myron once I'm processed?"

Mueller nodded again.

Daddy picked up his coat from the chair. He kept one arm around Lizzy as they all walked out the door.

# Chapter Twenty-Two

Lizzy stood on the sidewalk and watched the police car drive away in the fading light. Daddy sat in the passenger seat, next to Officer Mueller, his head held high. The car turned the corner and headed toward the town hall.

Lizzy trudged up the sidewalk to the porch. She hesitated at the bottom step. What was she going to say to Mama?

The front door burst open and Hank barreled down the steps, plowing into Lizzy before he realized she was there.

"Where have you been?" He grabbed her and pulled her up the steps.

She yanked out of his grip. "Where do you think I've been? I had to tell Daddy what you and Frank were going to do."

"Yeah, well, it's done," Hank said. "Mueller was here. We told him the truth. He went back out to Opa's house to pick up Pops and Myron."

"I know. I was there. They dropped me off."

Hank glanced down the street, but the police car was long gone.

"Daddy made me promise to tell Mama everything," Lizzy said.

"Yeah, well, that's done, too. You've got a lot of explaining to do. Mama is not happy."

Lizzy glanced at the open door. She could hear Frank and Mama talking in the kitchen.

"What did he tell you?" There was frustration, and fear, and something else in Mama's voice. Hope?

"I told you, we didn't get a chance to talk. I was caught off guard. I had so many things I wanted to ask, but I couldn't think of a one when I actually looked him in the eye."

Lizzy and Hank walked down the hall, their footsteps loud on the wood floor. Mama and Frank stopped talking.

Lizzy stepped through the kitchen door first, and she faced her mother without blinking. Mama looked at her for a long moment, then closed her eyes. "Shoes off."

Lizzy sat down to pull off her worn Mary Janes. Hank untied his shoes and slipped out of them. He picked up his pair and Lizzy's and carried them to the back porch.

"Lizzy ..." Mama stopped. "Why didn't you ..." She stopped again and sat down in the chair next to Lizzy. "Oh, honey." She held out her arms. Lizzy leaned over and sank into her mother's embrace. She cried silently as Mama stroked her hair.

Hank got a cup from the cupboard and poured himself some coffee. He pulled a chair out from the table and sat down.

Mama handed Lizzy the hanky she always kept tucked up her sleeve.

Lizzy blew her nose and sat back. "I'm sorry I didn't tell anyone. I didn't know what to do. Daddy asked me to wait until he could get Myron to a safe place. Myron's not—right." She offered the hanky back to Mama.

Her mother wrinkled her nose. "Keep it. And I know about Myron. Frank told me everything." She paused. "Your father is right to try and help him."

"It might be too late for that," Lizzy said.

"What do you mean?" Frank spoke for the first time, and Lizzy turned to him.

"Myron's gone."

"Gone?" Mama exclaimed. "Where did he go? How can he be gone?"

"I don't know. Daddy went to the Dinky Ditch to check his poles, and Myron was gone when he got home. That was right before we showed up."

"The guy's got one leg," Frank said. "He can't be far."

Lizzy shrugged. "Daddy couldn't find him. Officer Mueller is going to go back out and look, once Daddy is ... processed." The word was hard to say.

Mama put a hand to her forehead. "Your father's under arrest?"

Lizzy nodded.

Mama closed her eyes again and pinched the bridge of her nose, a familiar gesture that always meant she was trying to think.

She didn't think long. She put both hands on the table and pushed herself up and out of her chair. "Well, we have to help him. I'm not going to let anyone railroad your father into a jail cell. He had reasons for what he did."

She turned to her boys. "Hank, go find Opa. I want him to go with us. Of course, he can't walk. Frank, go ask Engle Ben if we can borrow his car again while I change into better clothes." Mama left the kitchen without waiting for any answers.

Hank was the first to speak. "She's going to help Pops." He raised one eyebrow. "I did not see that coming."

"Me either," said Frank. "But you heard her. Get Opa and tell him what's going on. I'll get the car."

Both boys left the room so quickly Lizzy had no time to volunteer to help or beg to go with them.

She trudged up the steps to her room, her thoughts jumbled. What was going to happen now? How could Mama ...

"Lizzy!"

Gene was peering out his bedroom door, his face barely visible. "Come here." His voice trembled with urgency. He stepped back into his room and held the door open.

Lizzy slipped inside. "What's wrong?"

Gene took a deep breath. "I know where Myron is."

"What? Wait—how do *you* know Myron's missing?"

"I just do, okay?"

Lizzy frowned. "Okay. So where is he?"

Gene's eyes were solemn. "He's in Goofy Ridge."

"Goofy Ridge?" Goofy Ridge was a bump in the road about five miles away. "What's he doing there?"

"He's waiting at the abandoned theater outside of town."

"How do you know that?"

"I know because I stole a car and drove him there."

# Chapter Twenty-Three

"*What?*" The word came out in a screech and Gene clapped his hand over her mouth.

She shoved his hand away, and her whisper was fierce. "I'm sorry, but you did what?"

"Okay, we didn't really steal it. Me and Otto took the Schimmelpfennings' car," Gene said. "Otto said if we got caught, he'd tell his grandfather he took the car on a joyride. But we got it back before anyone found out."

"Geeeeene ..." Lizzy's voice rose again, and she turned the one-syllable word into three.

"Calm down."

Lizzy took a deep breath and tried to count to ten. She made it to four. "How are you going to get Myron out of the Goofy Ridge Theater?"

"Otto said we could take the car again tonight, after everyone's asleep. We're going to pick Myron up and drive him to Indiana. His Uncle Albert lives right across the state line. We can drive there in a couple of hours. We'll leave around midnight and be back before sunup."

"How do you know where Myron's uncle is?"

"Myron told us."

"You mean he suddenly remembered? He hasn't been able to remember anything else for twenty years, but all of a sudden he remembers that?"

Gene shrugged. "I know he's got problems, but his mind was perfectly clear when he told us about Uncle Albert. He knows exactly how to get there."

Lizzy couldn't believe what she was hearing. "If you get caught tonight, Otto won't be able to claim he was on a joyride!"

"I know." Gene's eyes flickered with worry, but only for a moment. "We won't get caught."

Lizzy sat on the edge of the bed. "What made you decide to help Myron?"

"I went out to the farm to see Pops this afternoon. He wasn't there, but Myron was. We had a good talk. When he learned who I was, he told me he and Pops were trying to get to his family in Indiana. He said he didn't want to get Pops in any more trouble, and he had to leave Opa's house.

"I said I thought I could get a car and take him somewhere. We knew it would take Pops a while to check his lines, so I got back to town and told Otto what was going on. He got the car, and we got Myron to Goofy Ridge."

Gene paused. "You're not going to tell anyone, are you? Please don't, Lizzy."

Lizzy shook her head. "Gene, this is serious! Taking a stolen car to Indiana is way worse than a joyride to Goofy Ridge. What if the police stop you? What are you going to tell them?"

Gene sat next to her on the bed. "I don't know. But the car belongs to Otto's family, so if the police stop us, they won't press charges. But think about what will happen to Myron if Officer Mueller finds him. He'll either arrest him, or they'll stick him in the looney bin in Bartonville."

Lizzy shuddered. All the kids talked in whispers about getting sent to Bartonville. She didn't know anyone who had actually been there, so she didn't know if any of the stories were true. But if they were ...

"He was Pops's best friend. He *is* Pops's best friend," Gene continued. "We can't let that happen."

"Okay." She couldn't believe she was going along with this. "Be careful, all right? Does Otto know how to drive well enough to do this?"

Gene nodded. "Driving's easy. Otto and me have been out lots of times with Oscar."

"This is different."

"We'll be okay." He grasped her shoulder in one hand and gave it a comforting squeeze. "Think about it. We're not just doing this for Myron. We're doing this for Pops, too."

Lizzy didn't have an argument for that.

★★★

Mama, Opa, and the boys were gone a long time, so Lizzy and Gene made peanut butter and jelly sandwiches for supper and played games with Ginny. Lizzy couldn't focus, and she lost two games of Monopoly and three games of checkers.

*What's taking them so long? Why aren't they home? Will Daddy come home with them?*

Ginny wanted to play another game of checkers, but Gene faked a yawn, and Lizzy convinced her sister they needed to go to bed.

She herded Ginny upstairs, who was out and snoring in seconds. Lizzy lay in the dark, staring at the ceiling.

She heard the back door open and listened to the voices in the kitchen. It was only Joe and Jack, home from a late practice at the school.

Soon the front door opened, and Mama and the older boys were home. The voices faded down the hall, and Lizzy knew they were going to the kitchen to find something to eat.

Lizzy strained to hear her father's voice, but there was no sound of him. She knew people talked about heartache but she never thought it was a real thing until now. That spot in her chest actually hurt when she thought about Daddy sleeping on one of the hard cots she had seen in the jail.

Mama came upstairs and opened the door to check on her girls. Lizzy pretended to be asleep. She kept her eyes closed and breathed deeply until the door shut.

Time passed and the house grew quiet, but Lizzy still couldn't sleep. She flipped restlessly from her stomach to her back. Ginny stirred and mumbled into her pillow.

The clock downstairs began its soft chime and Lizzy counted the bongs. *Ten ... eleven ... twelve.* Twelve o'clock. The door to Gene's bedroom opened, so quietly Lizzy knew no one else would hear. There was no noise in the hall and then ... the third step from the bottom squeaked, and the sound seemed to echo through the house. She held her breath.

Nothing happened. No other bedroom doors opened, no one called down the stairs. She waited for the groan of the front door, but there was no sound. She slid out of bed and tiptoed to the window that looked down on the deserted street.

Lizzy could barely make out Gene's silhouette leaning against the big silver maple in the front yard. Gene turned and looked up at her window. He raised his hand in a wave. The Schimmelpfennings' blue DeSoto, headlights off, glided around the corner, and Gene stepped out from the tree. He was in the car and they were gone before Lizzy took a full breath.

She slipped back into bed and stared at the ceiling. *Please protect them, Lord. Please ...*

As she drifted into sleep, an image of Gene in the back of a police car suddenly formed, and she was wide awake again. Another slow drift and another image. This time Daddy was behind bars. Her eyes popped open and her heart beat hard in her chest.

She closed her eyes and tried again. This time Myron showed up in the Schimmelpfennings' car. *He's using his crutch to clutch.* Lizzy giggled sleepily at the unintended rhyme. Questions with no answers kept forming in her tired brain, but the one that kept repeating was *Where are they now? Where are they now?*

She must have dozed, because the sound of fingers scratching softly on the bedroom door brought her wide awake one more time.

Her heart pounded. *Someone knows Gene is gone. What do I do? What do I say?*

She tiptoed to the door and opened it, dreading whoever she would see.

It was Gene.

He leaned into the room and whispered in her ear, so close she could feel his breath. "Get dressed. You have to come with us."

The tremble in his voice and the fear in his eyes gave her no choice. She got dressed.

# Chapter Twenty-Four

Gene waited at the bottom of the stairs. Lizzy tiptoed down and stepped over the third step from the bottom.

She put a hand on Gene's arm. "What's going on?" she whispered. "Why do I have to go with you?"

"Myron's ... upset," Gene whispered back.

"How upset?"

"He's confused or something. I don't know. He thinks you're his sister Charlotte, and he doesn't want to go anywhere without you. We thought we could distract him and keep driving, but he started yelling and banging on the car door. We decided we had to come get you."

"Okay." Lizzy squared her shoulders. "Well, let's go. The sooner we leave the sooner we'll be back."

They slipped out the door and ran to the car. Lizzy opened the back door and slid across the seat. Gene slid in next to her.

Myron was in the front seat, and he turned and smiled at her. "Hi, Charlotte." His voice was gentle. "We're going to get you out of here."

Lizzy gave Gene a look. Gene shrugged.

"I thought we were taking you to see Uncle Albert," she said.

Myron nodded and turned back around. "We are. Uncle Albert's gonna watch out for both of us."

"Okay." Lizzy's breath fogged the window. She pulled her coat close around her and tucked her feet beneath her on the seat. *What will happen when he finds out I'm not staying at Uncle Albert's?*

Otto pulled smoothly away from the curb, and the car glided down the road. He turned the corner at William Street and shifted into second, only to tap the brakes and slow down.

"What's wrong?" Lizzy and Gene asked at the same time. Otto was easing over to the curb in front of the Beckers' house.

"I saw the police car cross the intersection up on Walnut," Otto whispered.

"Why you whispering, kid?" Myron asked. "He can't hear us. Sit here for a minute. See if he comes around. I can see his headlights, so we'll know if he turns back this way."

They waited in silence.

"Yep, he's coming back."

"Pull into the Beckers' driveway," Lizzy said.

"Why?" everyone asked.

"Otto, you know your brother goes out with Sarah Becker sometimes. If we're lucky, Mueller will think it's Oscar bringing Sarah home from a date."

"Right," Otto said.

"Do it!" Gene whispered. "He's at the corner. He'll be back up this street in no time."

Otto pulled into the Beckers' driveway and turned off the engine. They watched the police car turn the corner, and the same thought occurred to all of them at the same time. Lizzy, Gene, and Otto ducked down in their seats.

"Put your head down, Myron," Otto whispered.

Myron gave an exasperated sigh, but Lizzy watched his head disappear.

Lizzy squeezed her eyes shut and held her breath. They all listened as the police car rolled by the house without stopping. The sound of its engine faded.

She opened her eyes. "Do you think it's safe?"

Myron was sitting up straight, staring out the window. "It's safe. But we better get movin'."

Otto pulled out of the drive and headed back down the street. He kept the lights off until they were safely past Dora's Diner and headed out of town.

Lizzy spoke when they were several miles down the road. "How far is it to Uncle Albert's place, Myron? I mean, you do know where we're going, right?"

"Of course I do. You probably don't remember visitin' Uncle Albert and Aunt Hulda, do you? They live on a bluff right outside of Terre Haute." He chuckled softly. "They'll be real surprised to see you, Charlotte. You've gotten so big."

Lizzy glanced at Gene again, and he put a finger to his lips. "It'll be okay," he whispered.

Lizzy stared out the window. Sometimes the silhouette of a tree or a house drifted by in the dark. The steady hum of the engine was relaxing, and her eyes closed. She could hear the occasional murmured directions Myron gave to Otto, but they made no sense to her. Once she opened her eyes and saw snow floating down outside the window.

Lizzy didn't know how long she dozed like that, but sometime later she sat up, wide awake. The back wheels of the car were sliding sideways, and Otto was struggling to keep the car on the road.

In a calm but commanding voice, Myron said, "Turn the wheel to the right. No, your *other* right."

The car straightened out with a small shudder. Otto took a shaky breath.

"Good job, kid. You always turn in to a skid." Myron paused. "Never driven in snow before, huh?"

Otto gave a nervous laugh. "Uh, no."

"Ever *driven* before?"

"Oh, yeah, lots of times."

"Well, we're almost there, so you'll be able to relax here real quick."

Soon they turned down a dirt road. A mile later, they came to a small house on a bluff to the east. The house would have been invisible but for the full moon reflected off the snow around it. Otto turned into the drive.

"We're here." Myron turned in the seat and smiled at Lizzy. "Now do you remem ..." He stopped abruptly. "Where's Charlotte?" He peered at Lizzy in the darkness. "You're not Charlotte."

Gene leaned forward. "No, this is Lizzy, Myron. You remember her, right? We're Frank Richter's kids. Remember?"

Before Myron could answer, a light appeared in the window of the house. The front door opened, and a man appeared in the doorway.

Gene got out of the car. "I'm sorry it's so late," he called. "Are you Albert?"

The door opened wider, and the man stepped out on the porch. "No. My name's Roscoe. You lookin' for Albert Minser?"

"Yes," Gene replied.

"Albert Minser's dead."

## Chapter Twenty-Five

The silence in the car was so loud Lizzy thought she could hear the snow falling. Myron took a raspy breath. "Aw, shoot." His voice caught.

"Hulda Minser moved to town to live with her daughter," Roscoe continued. "Who are you?"

Gene walked up the porch steps. He and the man named Roscoe talked for several minutes, but Lizzy couldn't hear a word they said. Roscoe peered around Gene to look at the car. He shook his head and pointed up the road. A few more words were exchanged, and Gene offered his hand. Roscoe shook it, then he went inside and closed the door.

Gene slipped back into the car. There was a dusting of snow on his hair and jacket. "Roscoe gave me directions to the house where Hulda Minser is living. Let's go."

Otto sat with his hands on the wheel and didn't say anything.

"Otto? Let's go."

Otto turned to look at Myron. "I thought you said your uncle knew we were coming."

Myron shook his head. "I thought—well, I do remember he told me I was welcome any time."

"He's dead!" Otto's voice squeaked on the word dead, and he banged the wheel with one hand.

"I don't remember when I talked with him last," Myron admitted. "Mighta been a couple years ago. Maybe it was before the war."

Otto leaned over and put his forehead on the steering wheel. No one spoke for several moments.

Finally, Lizzy said, "Otto? Let's go. I mean, we have to try, right? Can we try?"

Otto nodded. He shifted the car into reverse and backed down the short drive. "I can't believe I stole my grandfather's car and came all this way just to find out ..." He didn't finish the sentence.

They headed back to the main road, and Gene gave him directions to a small town called Bellefleur, five miles away. The car hummed quietly down the road. When they arrived in Bellefleur, Gene directed him to the corner of Baker and Vine.

They all gaped. Even in the dark, it was obvious the large, well-kept, two-story house and fenced-in yard was owned by somebody with more money than anyone they knew. There was a large, wraparound porch with big columns, and the snow-capped trees around the yard made the house look prettier than any picture postcard Lizzy had ever seen.

Myron was the first one to speak. "Are you sure we got the right place?"

"Roscoe told me we were probably going to be surprised," Gene said. "I didn't know this was what he meant."

"Are you *sure* we got the right place?" Myron repeated.

"Pretty sure. Roscoe said the corner of Baker and Vine." Gene pointed silently to the street signs. Baker. Vine.

The soft glow of a lamp lit up a window on the first floor. Lizzy could see the outline of an older woman peering out at them. She moved away from the window, and a few seconds later the front door opened.

The woman appeared on the porch, wrapped in a dark housecoat, holding a shotgun.

All three children gasped.

Otto squeaked. "She's got a gun."

"She won't use it." Myron hesitated, and Lizzy saw his head tilt to one side. "Well, maybe she would. But only if you do something stupid." He chuckled. "So don't do anything stupid."

He grabbed his crutches, opened the car door, and eased his way out. When he was standing, he raised one crutch and shouted, "Hey, Aunt Hulda—it's me, Myron! Put the gun down, okay?"

"Who's calling me Aunt Hulda?"

"I'm calling you Aunt Hulda. Don't you recognize me? Myron? Myron Minser?"

The gun stayed where it was. "You're lying. Myron was killed in the war. Who are you?"

"It's me, Aunt Hulda. Honest," Myron said. "I know they told everyone I was dead. But look right here. Here I am. I'm kinda cold. Sure would like a glass of Glühwein right about now."

"What's Glühwein?" Otto whispered.

"Doesn't your grandfather drink Glühwein?" Gene whispered back.

"My grandfather doesn't drink."

Hulda's voice softened. "Myron?"

"Yep. It's me. I'm … I'm real sorry to hear about Uncle Albert. Who will I play Stern-Halma with at Christmas now?" Myron's voice cracked.

"What's 'Stern-Halma?'" Otto whispered.

Lizzy gave an exasperated sigh. "Are you sure you're German?"

Hulda rested the gun against the house, and she held out one hand. "Come here, honey. Let me look at you. Is it really you, Myron?"

Myron got from the car to the porch in record time. When he'd crutched his way to the top step, Hulda pulled him closer to the doorway to look in his face. "Oh, my." She started to cry.

The children watched Myron give her an awkward hug, one crutch holding him up and the other swinging in the air behind Hulda's back. After a few moments, he turned and motioned to the children. "Come here and meet Aunt Hulda."

Hulda's mouth opened and shut in apparent surprise when she saw three children step out of the car. "Oh, my." She picked her gun up. "Don't worry. It's not loaded." She pushed the front door open with her substantial hip. "Well, come on in and tell me your story."

The three children followed Myron into the house. Aunt Hulda fussed around them, taking coats and hats and getting them settled in chairs close to the fireplace.

Gene and Otto let Lizzy tell the story. An hour later, Myron was snoring on the couch before she finished the account of everything that had happened in the last week.

"My, oh my." Hulda pulled a beautiful, lace-covered hanky out of the sleeve of her house coat. Lizzy couldn't believe something so pretty had been shoved up the old woman's sleeve. She hoped Hulda wasn't going to blow her nose on it.

"That's some story." Hulda dabbed at her eyes with the hanky and tucked it back up her sleeve. "I don't know what your mama is gonna do to you when you get home, but I thank the Lord you took the chance to get Myron back to us." She watched Myron as he snored, and her eyes welled up. "Twenty-some years makes a big difference. He was a boy when I last saw him. But I'd recognize that grin anywhere." She pulled the hanky out and dabbed at her eyes again. "Thank you."

"He was Daddy's best friend," Lizzy told her. "We had to help him."

"Your daddy paid a price for his friend," Hulda said. "I know your family don't understand right now, but if that older brother of yours sees combat when he goes to war, it might start to make more sense. Men who soldier together have a special bond. Can't say I understand it, but I've seen it enough to know you can never shake it."

She turned to Otto. "Does your grandfather know you took his car?"

He blushed and shook his head.

"Well, then I figure the three of you have a tough day ahead. Best get back on the road. The snow's stopped so the drive home should be easier. You can probably be back before the sun's up if you don't have any trouble."

"I'm just hoping we get back before my father's up," Otto said.

"Mrs. Minser, I want to make sure you understand how much Myron's ... changed." Lizzy hesitated. "He's not the same as he was twenty years ago."

"Oh, honey, I could see that the minute I looked in his eyes." This time Aunt Hulda blew her nose with the hanky. "War can do awful things to a man. I've seen shell shock before. I know. But he's family. We'll take good care of him. That's what family does."

"Would you mind if our dad came to see him sometime?" Lizzy asked. "I mean, when he can. I know he'll want to keep in touch with Myron."

The old woman gave the children a warm smile. "He's welcome—you're all welcome—anytime."

They stood to leave, and the commotion caused Myron to stir. He opened his eyes and blinked several times. He sat up and yawned and rubbed his eyes and ran his hand over the stubble on his chin. He looked at all the children in turn, confusion on his face.

"What's goin' on?" When he saw Aunt Hulda, his eyes brightened and he tried to stand. But his crutches were across the room, and he flopped back to the sofa. "Aunt Hulda, what's goin' on? How'd I get here? Why's Lizzy here—and who are these boys ..."

The old woman moved to the sofa and put her arm around his shoulders. "Shush. We'll talk about all that later. These are Frank Richter's kids, and they brought you here to stay with me."

"Okay." Myron looked around the room. "Where's Frank?"

No one answered.

His voice rose. "Frank's in trouble, ain't he?" Myron looked from Lizzy to Gene to Otto. "He's in trouble 'cause he helped me, right? Am I right?"

Otto shifted and Gene didn't answer. Lizzy crossed the room and sat on Myron's other side on the sofa.

She took the man's rough, calloused hand in hers. "Daddy told me you saved his life during the war."

Myron swallowed hard. His Adam's apple bobbed up and down, and he closed his eyes.

"He thought you were dead," Lizzy continued, "but he never forgot what you did. When he discovered you were still alive, he had to help you." She paused and looked at Myron, willing him to open his eyes. He did, and tears started rolling down his cheeks.

"And yes, it did cause a lot of problems." She faltered and took a deep breath. "But I think things would have been worse if he hadn't tried. I'm glad he did. And he'll be happy to know you're going to be okay."

Myron nodded and swiped at the tears trickling down his face. "You tell him thank you for me, okay? Tell him

I'll be all right now. Tell him the good Lord's gonna take care of everything else."

Lizzy nodded. Myron squeezed her hand, then let go so he could reach inside his worn jacket. He pulled out a small paperback book, wiped the cover off on his sleeve and held the book out to Gene. "This is just about my all-time favorite story. Your daddy gave me this book. He knows I love Zane Grey. Now I want you to have it." He smiled. "He told me you love to read."

Gene took the book. "Thanks."

Lizzy leaned over and gave Myron a quick kiss on the cheek. "I'm glad you're home."

The three children gathered their coats and hats and gloves and prepared to go back out into the cold. Aunt Hulda walked them to the door.

She patted Otto's arm. "You drive careful, now, you hear me?"

Myron called to him from the sofa. "Remember, turn into the skid."

Aunt Hulda stood in the door and waved as Otto backed onto the road. Lizzy sat alone in the back seat, and she turned and watched out the window until the light from the beautiful house got swallowed up by the night.

# Chapter Twenty-Six

Lizzy was silent as they drove through the country. Otto and Gene talked so softly she had to sit forward to hear them. She put her chin on the cold leather of the front seat. She wanted to join the conversation, but her eyes kept drifting shut and the boys' voices faded.

Then Gene tapped her forehead with two knuckles, and she jumped. "I'm awake."

"Lie down. You're snoring."

She plopped over on her side without arguing. The drone of the engine lulled her back to sleep. When she opened her eyes again, the soft gray light of early morning revealed they were back in Black Hawk Grove. She yawned and sat up. They were sitting at a stop sign three blocks from their house.

Gene got out of the car and opened the back door for Lizzy. "We're going to walk home from here. We don't want the sound of a car waking anyone up. If we're lucky, everyone's still in bed. It's only six."

Lizzy and Gene trudged down the snow-covered sidewalk in silence. There was a soft glow ahead of them that grew brighter as they got closer to home. When they reached the corner of Paw Paw and Main Street, they both stopped. The Black Hawk Grove police car sat in front of their house, and there were lights on both floors.

Gene took a deep breath. "So much for sneaking home. This is going to be bad."

They walked up the steps, and the front door opened before they reached the landing. Frank crossed the porch in one stride and pulled Lizzy up the last step with both hands. He smothered her in a hug, then reached out and wacked Gene lightly on the back of the head before pulling him into the circle.

"You two are in so much trouble." The crack in his voice told Lizzy otherwise.

Mama came running out the door, and she grabbed Lizzy from Frank. She cried and hugged and scolded and hugged and cried some more.

"I'm sorry, Mama, I'm sorry." Lizzy tried to speak over her mother's tears. "We had to help him. We had to."

Mama finally took a breath, and Gene stepped up. "Don't be mad at Lizzy. I made her come with us."

Mama pulled Gene into a hug, and sniffled one last time. She pulled a hanky out of her sleeve and wiped her nose and eyes. "Well, both of you, come down to the dining room. We've got a lot to talk about. Everyone is waiting."

Everyone?

Lizzy followed her mother through the swinging door. Opa and Hank sat on opposite sides of the dining room table, each with a twin next to them. Opa's face sagged in relief when he saw Lizzy and Gene. Hank shook his head and closed his eyes.

Lizzy finally realized how frightened everyone had been. Even the twins looked troubled, although Joe whispered something to his brother, drawing a snicker from Jack. Opa made a growling sound, and Jack sobered up.

Lizzy sucked in a breath when she realized the family wasn't alone. Officer Mueller, his eyebrows pulled down into a caterpillar again, sat with Otto's grandfather and father. Cap Campbell sat apart from the group in a chair he'd pulled into the corner.

Officer Mueller rose from his seat. He looked at Lizzy and Gene, and the caterpillar danced right above his nose. "Where have you been, and how did you get home?"

Neither Lizzy nor Gene answered. There was no way they were going to tell the officer where Myron was staying. And Lizzy was sure Otto's family knew what they had done, but she wasn't going to give up Otto. Neither was Gene.

The officer tried again. "Can I assume Myron Minser is somewhere safe?"

Both children nodded.

Mueller had one more question. "Did you steal the Schimmelpfennings' car to get him there?"

"No." Both of them answered, and Lizzy looked sideways at the Schimmelpfennings. The two Oscars exchanged a glance. They rose from their seats.

"We'll be going home," Oscar Jr. said. "Pretty sure the car will show up soon. We'll let you know."

Mueller nodded. "Do you need a ride?"

"*Nein, danke,*" said old Oscar. "A walk in the snow will do us good."

In a more ominous tone, Oscar Jr. said, "We need the time to cool down."

Lizzy wondered when they would see Otto again. Oscar Jr. pushed the swinging door open and held it for his father. Lizzy risked a glance at old Oscar, and he gave her a wink.

Lizzy pulled a chair out from the table, and Gene sat down next to her. No one said a word.

Mama broke the silence. "I wish you hadn't felt the need to do this on your own. We could have worked something out."

Lizzy and Gene stayed quiet.

Mama continued. "However, having said that, I'm glad you took the chance you did to help Myron. He is still your father's best friend."

Jack's mouth dropped open. Joe looked indignant. "What? That's it? They're not in trouble? They're not grounded?"

The other siblings started laughing, and Mama rolled her eyes and shook her head.

Even Opa had a reluctant grin on his face. "Settle down. They've got a ways to go before they catch up with you two."

"Thank you, Mama." Lizzy hesitated, reluctant to ask the obvious. "Where's Daddy?"

Mama glared at Officer Mueller. "I can only assume he is still in the lockup."

Officer Mueller coughed. "I will have to review the charges against him."

Cap leaned forward. "Okay, this is where I come in. It's been about a month since the police charged Frank with assaulting the guards at the asylum. You all know the story, but I don't think Officer Mueller does." He turned to the policeman. "Myron was the one who actually committed the assault. So the doctor sent Myron straight to solitary, and prescribed a new treatment— shock therapy." Cap shook his head. "It's drastic, and the results are questionable, sometimes catastrophic. Frank and I agreed we couldn't let that happen. Your father came back to get Myron out of there. I left a few doors unlocked to make things easier for him."

Officer Mueller interrupted him with a frown. "It would appear you should both be under arrest."

Cap shrugged. "Maybe. But I don't think you'll find anyone who will charge us. I'm here because the asylum was closed down two weeks ago for medical malpractice and gross negligence."

Mama's back stiffened and one hand went to her throat. "Malpractice and negligence?" she repeated, her voice faint. "That's what Myron's been dealing with?"

Cap nodded. "But that's over now. Thanks to you two"—he looked at Lizzy and Gene—"he's safe with family. And since the asylum has been closed, I think the police will be willing to drop the charges against Frank." He spoke again to Officer Mueller. "If I can go back to the village hall with you and make a couple of phone calls, we should be able to get everything straightened out."

Mueller nodded. "Under the circumstances, I will release Frank until all is settled." He studied the sober faces around the table. "I truly hope this helps."

Cap stood up, and the two men left the dining room. The front door opened and shut.

Frank went to the kitchen and came back with four coffee cups looped through the fingers of one hand and the coffee percolator in the other.

He set cups in front of Mama and Opa and filled them, then offered one to Hank. Hank shook his head. Frank filled one for himself and sat down.

All the siblings were staring at him, and he shrugged and smiled. "KP duty."

Soft laughter around the table faded quickly.

"So, what now?" Frank asked.

Hank took a ragged breath. "I know you said it's not my decision to make, Mama, but I don't know if I'm ready for Pops to come home."

Mama reached out and took Hank's hand. "I'm not sure I'm ready either."

"How do we know—how can we ..." Hank shook his head and covered his eyes.

"James 1:5, son," Mama said.

Hank repeated the verse they all had memorized. "'If any of you lack wisdom, let him ask of God, that giveth to all men liberally and upbraideth not; and it shall be given him.'" He took another long breath and rubbed his eyes. "Okay. I'll ask."

"We'll all ask," Mama said. "We all need wisdom on this one."

"In the meantime ..." Opa said, "there might be a way to make things easier."

Everyone waited.

Opa coughed, then drummed his fingers on the table. "Not sure I'll say all this just right, but I'll try." He cleared his throat again and took a breath. "Don't think I'm not grateful for your help, Annie. I know I couldn't stay at the farm by myself a couple months ago, but I'm better now. And I'm used to my privacy. Six kids ... well ..." He paused and looked around the table. "You can be a real handful."

Everyone looked at the twins, and Joe nudged Jack. "Why's everyone looking at us?"

"They're looking at you," Jack replied.

"Anyways," Opa continued, "what if I moved back to the farm and Frank moved in with me? At least for the time being?"

Mama reached out and took his hand. Her eyes teared up, but she nodded. "That sounds like a good idea. For the time being." She squeezed his rough, gnarled fingers. "We'll miss you."

He squeezed back. "That'll give you space to work things out."

"There's a lot to work on," she agreed.

The front door opened, and the sound froze everyone in their seats. They heard first one shoe, then another, drop on the rug by the door. Familiar footsteps padded down the hall. The dining room door swung open, and Daddy stood in the doorway.

"*Schatzi.*" The word slipped out before Mama could stop it. She bit her bottom lip, then stood up and held out one hand.

Daddy came in the room and around the table. He took her hand and held it to his cheek, his eyes closed for several long moments. When he opened them, he looked around the table at each of his children, then back at Mama. "Ginny?"

"Still asleep."

He nodded. He turned to Lizzy and Gene. "Mueller told me what you did. Thank you."

Gene's smile nearly split his face, and he didn't seem to care about the tears that wet his cheeks. "You're welcome, Pops."

Lizzy just grinned and gave her father a brief wave. He winked.

He turned to Joe and Jack. Both were blinking hard. Joe elbowed Jack and got an elbow in return.

"Hi, boys," Daddy said.

"Hey, Pops." They replied in perfect unison, and Daddy choked back a laugh or a sob—Lizzy wasn't sure which.

He turned last to his two oldest sons. They watched him silently. Daddy tried twice to speak, but no words came out. Finally, he found just the right ones. "I'm sorry."

Frank's expression softened, and he gave a brief nod. Hank made a noise, deep in his chest, covered his eyes.

"Son."

Hank looked up.

"Take your time. Take all the time you need."

Hank nodded.

Mama eased into her chair, and she patted the empty seat between her and Opa. Daddy sat next to her. She studied his face. Her hopeful expression battled with her sober eyes. "We have a lot to talk about."

Daddy nodded. "I know. I'll do whatever I can to make things right with each one of you, no matter how long it takes. No matter what it takes."

He swallowed hard. "I suspect it's gonna take a healthy dose of the grace of God." He looked around the table at his children. "I'm going to ask him to show me how to be a father again."

Opa, ever practical, spoke first. "In the meantime, I bet you could use a cup of coffee."

Daddy placed a hand on his father's shoulder. "Did you make it?"

Opa laughed out loud. "Of course not."

"Good. Then I'd love some coffee."

Reluctant smiles and a soft chuckle or two went around the table, and Lizzy thought her heart would burst.

*Thank you, Lord.*

# Chapter Twenty-Seven

The whole family gathered at the bus stop to see Frank Jr. off. Uncle Charlie, Aunt Meg, and all the cousins were there. Frank shook hands all around with the boys. He hugged Elinor and Marianne, and he gave Aunt Meg a hug and a kiss that made her cry. Uncle Charlie pressed something into his hand, and Lizzy was pretty sure it was a five-dollar bill.

Then they faded back, and Mama, Daddy, and the rest of the family crowded in close. No one knew what to say, but someone had to start.

"I don't care how busy you are, you write to Mama, okay?" Hank's voice was rough. "She'll need to hear from you."

Frank wrapped his brother in a bear hug. Then the other boys grabbed him and hugged him, and there was lots of back slapping.

"Behave yourselves," Frank said to the twins. They both nodded. For once neither one had a smart remark.

Joe swiped at his eyes, and Jack nudged him. "Stop it."

Frank smiled at Gene. "You're going to be something, little brother. I can't wait to see what it is."

Gene smiled back. "Neither can I."

Frank knelt in front of Ginny. She buried her head in his shoulder.

"Hey," he said. "I'll be back in no time."

"I'll practice my knuckleball every night. You'll be proud of me."

Frank gave his youngest sister a kiss. "I'm proud of you, no matter what. But keep practicing."

He stood and turned to Lizzy. "You're turning into a beauty, Squirt. Inside and out. Don't let it go to your head. Keep those boys in line, okay?"

Lizzy blushed. She nodded and hugged Frank hard, and she didn't cry. "I'll write you every week."

Opa shook his hand and gave him a small, worn book—Oma's New Testament. "You're in my prayers, son."

Frank tucked the book in his front pocket. "Thanks, Opa."

Then he hugged Mama for a long, long time. When he finally let go, she stepped back and placed one hand gently on his cheek. "Come home to me."

Frank reached out a hand to his father. Daddy shook it.

"No matter what happens," Daddy said, "I'll be here when you come home."

Frank nodded. "I know. I'm counting on it."

The bus driver tooted his horn, and Frank grabbed his rucksack. He took a window seat and waved at everyone as the bus belched smoke and pulled away.

Daddy had one arm around Mama, and she leaned against him. Everyone else watched the bus, but Lizzy watched Mama and Daddy.

*No matter what it takes.*

Lizzy turned back to the bus and waved until it was out of sight.

## *About the Author*

**Leanne Lucas** is a graduate of the University of Illinois with a degree in teaching English and a minor in narrative writing. She is the author of eight middle-grade novels, *The Addie McCormick Adventures*, originally published by Harvest House, Inc. The series was also published by the German publishing company, Christliche Verlagsgesellschaft Dillenburg. Currently, Finding Christ Through Fiction has republished the first three books in the series. She has also written a variety of fiction and nonfiction for Christian magazines for children (*Dash, Venture*), as well as Sunday School materials for David C. Cook and Thomas Nelson.

She recently retired after eighteen years as a writer for the College of Agricultural, Cultural, and Environmental Sciences and the Department of Agricultural and Biological Engineering at the University of Illinois.

Dear Reader:

If you enjoyed *When Skies are Gray*, I'd love to hear from you. You can find me on Facebook at https://www.facebook.com/leannelucaswriter or on my website at https://leannelucas.com/

Writers are thrilled with messages and reviews--if you'd take a minute to drop a line or two on Amazon or Goodreads, I'd very much appreciate your thoughts about Lizzy, Ginny, Opa, Frank, and the rest of the family.

Made in the USA
Monee, IL
22 November 2022